To
My wife, Patty
My mother, Peggy
My dear friends, Ms. Clara and Ms. Dora

Thank you for teaching me, each in your own way, the
enormous value of having a secret meeting place.

I thank You for the bitter things.
They've been a friend to grace.
They've driven me from the paths of ease
To storm the secret place.

— *Florence White Willett*

Acknowledgments

THANKS TO Wes Yoder of Ambassador Agency for matching Mark and me.

Thanks to Mike Cox of Alpha Advertising, in Sidell, Illinois, for creating the cover design and to Ed Bowman, for a wonderful cover photograph. Thanks to Diana Donovan of Celo Valley Books in Burnsville, North Carolina, for working with Mike on the cover, for creating the page design, and for helping me edit the manuscript.

Last but certainly not least, deep and heartfelt thanks to my writing associate, Mark Smeby. This book is as much from your heart as it is from mine.

FOREWORD

AT THE OPENING of *The Secret Meeting Place,* fear and routine have controlled Lars and his fellow villagers for as long as anyone remembers. But Lars has grown tired of merely going through the motions of life, and he decides to break this tradition.

The mountain that stands at the edge of the village of Berglund has been seen only as a monument to danger—the danger associated with taking risks. It is a convenient excuse to anyone who might think of pursuing bigger dreams.

Lars comes to see that mountain as a road to new possibility, and he dares to explore. Its solitary slopes offer him the opportunity to meet Solveig, who helps him discover truths that bring him to fulfillment. Through Lars the unlikely hero, Berglund is changed.

Come with him as he climbs to Solveig's secret meeting place and listens to her wisdom. Journey with him as he learns how to become a special husband, father, friend, and leader. You may find yourself becoming one of many whom Lars has inspired.

O_{NE}

THE STREETS WERE COATED with an early morning silence in the quaint village of Berglund (whose name means *mountain land*). The sun was beginning to peek through the trees on the east edge of the village. Streams of smoke rose from the chimneys of assorted houses, all of which were positioned near the roads, in order to ease the villagers' walk to and from their jobs.

Berglund's one-room schoolhouse was quiet for the weekend, but primed for another week of classes that would begin the following day. Located north of the main road so that it would not disrupt any business activity, the school had plenty of room for a playground and sporting field.

Berglunders were preparing for the day in, most likely, the exact same way they began every Sunday. Routine was the essence of Berglund. For as long as anyone could remember, the motto of the village had been "If it worked yesterday, it is good enough for today."

Berglunders would walk to church along dusty roads with deep ruts in them. These same routes were used by the same villagers each day. Tired, obedient feet never once swerved from the paths they trod between home and work—never once thought about taking a detour or trying something new just for the fun of it.

The inhabitants of Berglund walked with determination to

their destinations. Without truly noticing any chance encounter, they would feel lucky if they got a "Nice weather we're having!" or a "How are the kids?" out of someone passing by. But they certainly did not expect such a comment. Everybody in Berglund was sure they already knew everybody else. They knew what the other villagers did for work and fun, and most likely why they did it. Why pry? This "understanding" significantly cut down on needless conversation, they thought. It was not recognized as the habit it was: one that had led the people of Berglund into an inability to care very deeply about anybody else or what they did.

For jobs, there was no question of what people would do in life. Children would follow in the footsteps of their parents: The children of farmers would be farmers; the children of bankers would be bankers; the daughter of the teacher would unquestionably be the next teacher for the village.

These unwritten rules had been handed down through the centuries and followed without exception. Any new idea would be greeted with suspicion.

And it was the same with the written rules. The mayor of the village had been elected solely to make sure that those written laws were never changed. The ways things were done had been good enough for hundreds of years, so no one saw any need to change anything.

This morning, as on every Sunday morning, the villagers put on their best clothes and made an appearance at the local church. For adults, an appearance meant sitting quietly in their usual seats for nearly forty-five minutes. For children, it meant doing their best to stay awake. Pastor Sundqvist usually preached about the "don'ts"—something about this sin or that, or about what a horrible place Hell was—and then everyone went home. If asked, the people of Berglund would say they were religious because they attended church regularly, but no one ever seemed inspired to seek God directly or to apply His love to their lives.

The ritual today was no different. Lars Hansen sat quietly

The Secret
Meeting Place

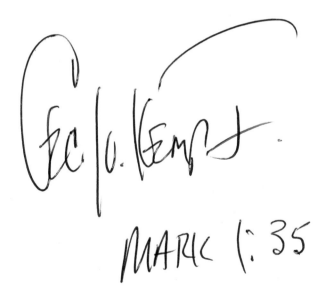

MARK 1: 35

The Secret
Meeting Place

CECIL O. KEMP JR.
AND
MARK SMEBY

w

The Wisdom Company
Franklin, Tennessee

Published by:

THE WISDOM COMPANY
P.O. Box 681351
Franklin, TN 37068-1351
Telephone: 1-800-728-1145
Fax: 1-615-791-5836
E-mail: cecil@hopestore.com

Cecil's books are sold on the Internet at www.hopestore.com and in local bookstores and gift shops. Bookstores or gift shops that don't already carry his books can order them from FaithWorks/National Book Network by calling toll free 1-877-323-4550.

ISBN 1-893668-22-3
Library of Congress Catalog Card Number 00-00000

with his two eldest children—eight-year-old Jens, and Erik, who was six—occasionally tapping the backs of their heads with his hand to keep them awake. Hell is generally an interesting topic for youngsters to hear about, but even that gets boring after hearing it this many times. (It had been fifty-seven times for Jens and twenty-seven times for Erik, to be exact.)

Before the service, no Berglunder had bothered to ask Lars why his wife, Lena, and their three-year-old daughter, Inge, weren't there this particular morning. Lars hadn't expected such a question. Nor had he questioned who should go to church with the boys and who should stay home with their ill daughter. He was used to things as they were, and so was Lena, who followed Berglund expectations. She was a patient woman, not prone to voicing complaint, and dedicated to the benefits of routine. Her proficiency in raising the three Hansen children left Lars feeling free from the duties of helping to care for them. His work, he was sure, was outside the home.

Lars was a hammersmith who worked very hard to provide for his family, even though it never seemed to be enough. His father had been a hammersmith, as had the father of his father. The men in Lars' family had, of course, always been hammersmiths. And they also told themselves that it was the best job in the village.

When Lars was not working as a hammersmith, he was at home constructing additional rooms for his house, rooms that his family never used. But Lars had not noticed why they weren't used: Lena and the children liked the rooms they already had. They wanted more of Lars—not more rooms!

This Sunday, Lena was at home caring for Inge, who had an extremely high fever. It was from one of many illnesses that the child seemed to fall prey to so easily.

Inge's bedsheets were soaking wet with perspiration, yet she kept shivering as if she were freezing cold. Her mother had a pan of cool water beside the bed, and she used it frequently. After wetting a towel in it, Lena would tenderly lay the cool cloth across her daughter's forehead. Relaxing the little girl in this way seemed all her mother could do.

Young Inge had had polio before she was one, and was unable to walk. She usually went anywhere the family went, though. For one of her parents would either carry her, or wheel her around in a wheelchair that Lars had made for her.

The other villagers never stared or whispered when Inge was brought by. In fact, not once had anyone asked about her condition when they'd talked to Lars or Lena. This was something the Hansens attributed to the village's little "understanding."

Sitting in church that morning with his two sons, Lars worried about Inge's health. But he did not think to pray for her. He decided to begin working even harder on a special room for her, one she would certainly like enough to want to use. He visualized each of the room's details as he kept an eye on his sons.

And when it was time to leave that day, he spoke to no one about his daughter's latest illness . . . or of his worry . . . or of his plans to build her a new room.

The Hansens buried their youngest child, their only daughter, late on Tuesday afternoon as the sun slipped behind the mountain. Lars found himself filled with the anger of helpless regret. What could he have done to make Inge's short life better than it had been?

"As we lay our precious Inge into the ground, we watch the sun disappear behind the mountain," Lars said solemnly during the private family burial. "But tomorrow will arrive soon, and with it a new sun and another day to . . . love those around us."

Lars's rote words gave no hint of his struggle inside. As the family trudged home, Lars became convinced that, for him, at least, something had to change.

He did not understand why his heart burned with a grief that seemed deeper than the sorrow of losing his daughter (however great that pain was). As the days passed, he decided that the agonizing ache was over an idea he could no longer silence. It was the idea that he might possibly be losing his own life. Not through ill health, but in the routine of the mundane, which he and the other villagers had perfected.

This ache was like a wound that would not heal. And it brought with it searing questions like: Was there something more important than working and dying? Was it at all possible to taste the wine of a sweeter berry—or swim the waters of a warmer spring? Could joy be deeper, love purer, or life richer? These were questions that brought with them feelings Lars didn't know what to do with.

On a Wednesday not long after Inge's death, Lars went to his shop as usual. He hoped that working would still the jumble of guilt and anger in his head. That morning, though, he had to go to work twice, because when he first got there, he couldn't find his shop keys. After stomping home and retrieving them from his other pair of pants, he returned to work. But he found no comfort there. No task went well, it seemed.

The following Sunday, he and a silent Lena went to church with the boys as usual. Lars couldn't think what to say when Lena wistfully sighed during the sermon and whispered to him that part of her still clung to the fantasy that Inge was at home waiting for their return. The sermon, which today was about the importance of continuing religious tradition, was no help. Lars noticed that his mind was repeating angry questions as though looking for something—anything—to be angry at. He began to think, finally, that it was avoiding a very dangerous thought: Lars wondered if he might be angry at this God he barely knew.

Things were quiet in the Hansen home that evening. After the family ate their supper, the boys decided to go to bed earlier than usual, allowing their parents some time alone. Lars and Lena sat wordlessly by the hearth, unable to do more than hold hands for a moment. The grief they both felt, but had difficulty expressing to each other, came out of entirely different places.

Lena missed seeing Inge's face, holding her close, taking care of her. Lena felt that she had received so much more love from Inge than she had ever given her daughter. She missed the presence of that love. And she was trying to relive it, not only by caring for her sons, but by renewing her love for her husband. She wasn't sure how to do this, however, since their routine called for Lars to be hardly ever at home.

Lars' pain came out of a regret that burned relentlessly within. He knew he regretted spending so little time with his only daughter. But since Inge's death, he knew there was something else wrong as well. And not knowing what it was left him more silent than ever, unable to express his confusion to Lena, the woman he most wanted to share comfort with.

Lars tried to hold Lena in bed that night. He could feel his wife's longing for him. But instead he tossed and turned, and finally, in the middle of the night, he got up and decided to go to his closest friend, Tomas, for advice.

Tomas' commitment to the status quo was viewed as the village standard. In fact, that commitment of his, and his kind way of applying it to situations, was why Tomas had been serving as mayor for several years now. He was known to be up many nights, often going over recent events, to be sure that the laws—written and unwritten—were being followed.

Tomas was not only Lars' best friend, he was respected in Berglund as having gathered much kindhearted wisdom through study and experience. Lars hoped that his friend would have some advice for him on this restless night.

After knocking at Tomas' door, Lars waited for what felt like an eternity.

Tomas finally appeared, said, "Lars?" and began the polite comment, "A fine night to be out for a walk—" But he broke off when he saw how agitated his friend was.

"Do you mind if I come in?" Lars asked, arms crossed as though hugging himself.

"No, please do!" Tomas said, and he ushered Lars into the living area of his home. "So sorry about Inge. . . ." Tomas offered in an unpracticed effort to show sympathy.

But Lars didn't seem to hear the words. Instead he said bluntly, "Tomas, do you ever just stop what you're doing and think, 'Why am I doing this?' "

His friend stood there with a confused look, trying to understand the question.

Lars continued, desperate to pry into Tomas' mind.

"Do you ever think that . . . that maybe there is something else out there besides the day-to-day things we do?" Lars paced around the edge of the hooked rug as he tried to describe what he was feeling. "It's like we're trapped into thinking that life is only *this* good"—he held up his hand and pinched his thumb and index finger together—"when . . . when we're all wishing things were . . . better!"

"Are you feeling all right, Lars?" Tomas asked with as much compassion as he could muster. (He couldn't think of any other way to respond.)

"No! I'm not!" Lars answered back, the volume of his voice greatly increased. "I am *not* at all 'all right,' thinking this is all there is! There has got to be a better way to live life! It cannot be only about doing what's expected and then . . . dying!"

But, though Lars passionately tried to explain his growing hunger for understanding, his effort failed. Tomas could not see past the way he had done things his whole life. He was too sure of exactly what he needed to do to keep everything in order.

After listening to Lars for several minutes, Tomas finally responded, "Lars, I wish I could help you. I really do. But I only know that *I'm* happiest when I'm doing what I know I need to do."

This was the last straw for Lars. "You cannot see anything except what's right in front of your face!" he shouted. "I want to see what I cannot see with my eyes! I want to hear what I cannot hear with my ears!" he demanded, sounding just a little like an angry child. "Oh, Tomas, I thought you were my friend! Why don't you understand?" With that, Lars stood up and ran out of the house.

Tomas' yard was in shadow. In his haste, Lars stumbled on

the edge of the wall that stood at the end of Tomas' yard—a wall that had been constructed to protect the house from rising water (even though there was no river or stream nearby)—and fell flat on his face. After catching his breath, Lars got up onto his knees, brushed himself off, and shifted his gaze down the length of the road. He had never seen the view from this perspective.

The outlines of houses and trees were accentuated in the moonlight. It was amazing how, if you weren't standing, the trees along the sides of the street seemed to point toward the mountain at the edge of Berglund. Seen this way, the mountain sat squarely at the end of the road. Or at what would have been the end of the road, if the road had gone that far. The villagers had stopped using that part of the road so many years ago, though, that, with lack of use, the trees and undergrowth now made a pseudo-end just past the house of the village treasurer.

Tonight, the moon shone on the peak of the mountain, causing it to glow with an intensity Lars had never seen in his entire life. He gazed at its silent, rugged beauty for some time.

Two ❧

PEOPLE IN THE VILLAGE had stopped looking past, or even at, the mountain generations ago. It was rumored in Berglund that the mountain would swallow anybody who ventured up its ragged stone trails. Because of stories about ancestors who'd lost their lives while climbing, Berglunders saw the mountain, at its worst, as a gigantic monument to the danger attached to any kind of risk taking. At its best, it blocked their view of what lay to the west, and caused the sun to disappear too early each day.

After returning home from visiting Tomas, Lars could not forget how the rugged, glowing peak had seemed to point to the heavens, as though inviting him to reach for things higher and greater. Had it been an answer to his demands? If so, Lars thought, the mountain was not merely something standing in the way of seeing grander sunsets, not simply something that kept the village in shadow from late afternoon on. It was also a giant challenge course to something new.

Lars had always been one who, like the other villagers, never considered a trip up the side of the mountain. He hadn't wanted to lose his life as the victims in village stories had. But after losing Inge, and after seeing the glowing mountaintop in front of Tomas' house, Lars found himself ready to try anything new.

The following evening after dinner, while everyone in the

village was nestled in their homes, Lars gently told Lena what he had decided. He would take a backpack and then proceed up the mountain sometime after midnight, while the moon was still high. Unclear where he might be going or what he might need, he settled on taking water, three biscuits from the previous night's meal, a blanket, a knife, a handful of leaves from his yard, and a bundle of matches.

Already disturbed by Lars' behavior since Inge's death, and frightened now by his completely uncharacteristic plan to climb a mountain she had been taught to fear, Lena clung to the commonplace—she said nothing to Lars about his plan, but turned back to her task of cleaning up the supper dishes.

Later, as he started his hike, Lars contemplated his anger and frustration with God. He thought about how, even though he had gone to church his whole life and learned all the stories, God had not healed his daughter. Why shouldn't Lars be angry with Him? Wasn't He supposed to be ultimately in control of everything that happened?

Lars hoped to find some kind of answer on the ridges of the mountain. He hoped, too, that some kind of supernatural navigation would keep him from getting lost and would lead him to where the answers lay. If he died on the mountain, so be it, he told himself. If he lived and didn't find any answers, the hike would still be worth the risk. Because at least he would have tried. And trying had to be better than letting this rage inside him continue to burn.

That first night Lars found the overgrown road to the foot of the mountain fairly easy to hike. But the path up the side of the mountain was rocky and, in the shadows, difficult to follow. He quickly learned how difficult it was to see where to put his feet. Disoriented, Lars decided to eat two of his biscuits and take a nap in the section of thick brush he found himself in. There was no place to build a fire, but there was just enough room to spread out his blanket.

He awoke several hours later. The moon was setting and

the sky was pearl gray. Lars rose, put his blanket away, ate his last biscuit, and drank some of the water he'd brought. Then he resumed his walk.

Not far up the trail, he stopped to pick some berries. Suddenly he noticed that, on the other side of the bushes, an old woman was kneeling with her face to the ground.

She was saying, ". . . and, God, I pray that You will continue to accomplish *Your* will in my life, not my own. Bring to me whomever you desire me to meet, and keep me from those who—" At that, she apparently heard Lars rustling a branch of the small bush he was crouched behind. "—from those who would do me evil. Amen." She sat silent for a minute.

The quiet fell heavily on Lars, who wanted to see her next move.

The woman sat halfway up, still crouched on her knees, her hands resting on her thighs. Without as much as a glance she whispered, "I have been waiting for you." She waited another moment, then turned and looked in Lars' direction.

A warmth fell over his entire body when he looked into her eyes.

"For me? Waiting for me?" he cautiously asked, stepping out from behind the bush.

"Today is the day for which you have been preparing your entire life," she intoned with a grace and confidence that Lars had never heard. "Welcome to my secret meeting place."

Lars had no idea what to say. He stood as still as a tree, until his hands began to shake.

"God wants to use you to awaken the slumbering souls around you," the woman stated simply.

Lars did not understand why *he* would be chosen. He was *angry* with this God Who, he was sure, had taken his Inge. He, Lars, was only a hammersmith, and had left his wife in a time of deep sorrow to seek an . . . answer?

"But why—?" he began to ask the woman.

She interrupted. "Because you seek answers. Because you chose to climb the mountain—even though you've been told it's dangerous. God has promised that whoever dares to step out in faith will be met with help. That help is where I come in."

Lars suddenly realized that this situation might be something he wasn't going to like. "Who says I even *want* to awake these sleeping people, or whatever you say I'm supposed to do?"

"I have wisdom to give you that will enable you to accomplish your task," she replied in a gentle tone of voice, finally standing up.

Lars' feeling of being cornered began to fade.

"That sounds great, but who *are* you, exactly?"

The mysterious woman said with graceful conviction, "My name is Solveig. Trust me, I will tell you more about myself over time. But first, you need to get to know yourself. Why not start by looking around?" She stepped back and gestured toward the valley.

Lars noticed that the sun was rising on Berglund, casting light—and long morning shadows—across the town. The view from even this relatively low spot on the mountain allowed him to see things he had never noticed before. He saw his own house, with its empty addition tacked on to the back. He saw something else, too. In building it, he had thought he was doing what he was supposed to do to care for his family. But . . . and the thought suddenly came to him oh so clearly: His self-righteous busy-ness had not been for them at all! It had been for his own sense of self. And it had, in reality, *hurt* his family, not helped them. Because it had kept him from them when they needed his presence.

As if she knew what he was thinking, Solveig said gently, "You are going to see many things you have never seen before. If you are willing to listen and grow."

Though the woman seemed so gracious and good and spoke so gently, Lars' fear of being out of control returned. He was just about to refuse her invitation when Solveig took a step toward him and reached out her weathered hand. He did not retreat.

Instead Lars felt his hand rise toward the old woman's,

without his really willing it to do so. When their fingers touched, Lars immediately felt a deep warmth course through his body. He closed his eyes as they stood motionless, hands locked, and tried to absorb some of this new energy. It made him feel understood, loved. . . . He didn't ever want to let go.

"To know the way up *and down* the mountain," she whispered after a while, "ask the One who made it."

Lars now knew that this gracious stranger was not to be feared. And that the answers he was looking for would soon be found.

THREE ❧

SOLVEIG'S SECRET MEETING PLACE on the side of the mountain was obviously not a secret to everybody. It was simply a
place where the path widened to nearly ten feet. Travelers
attempting to climb the mountain throughout the centuries
had used this spot to rest, and sometimes even to spend the
night. As Lars had already discovered, there was a beautiful
view of the countryside below. There was also enough open
space to see the sky above, and a slight, rocky overhang that
could protect travelers from the elements.

The birds had already begun their early morning chirping,
and were flying over Lars and the old woman as if supervising
their activities. Solveig had let go of Lars' hand and was standing with hands folded, looking him over. Casually she said,
as if she had done this kind of leading her whole life, "Let us
figure out who you are."

"That's what I've been wondering lately!" Lars chuckled.

Solveig grinned a big toothy grin and locked eyes with
Lars. "Before we can fill you up with good things," she said,
and then she leaned closer to Lars and whispered, "we have
got to find the bad stuff you have to get rid of!"

Lars, fearful of losing his most charming characteristics,
asked, "Do I get to decide what stays and what goes?"

"Funny you should ask," she answered with an all-knowing gleam in her eye, which Lars knew he was going to have to get used to. "I will tell you a secret."

Lars loved secrets. He waited eagerly.

"The secret to finding what you are looking for is letting go," Solveig said slowly. "This is a hard lesson for all of us. There are things you will hold on to for the rest of your life—things you absolutely need to let go of. But trusting that the benefit of letting go will be greater than the security of holding on to them—that is where you will find the deepest satisfaction in this life. The deepest joy."

"Joy. Is that what I'm after?" Lars found the simplicity of the words difficult to believe.

"We are all after something," she smiled. "And what is better? Listen: To get something, you have to choose it. Which means choosing *not* to seek what gets in the way. It is time to decide what the very best thing is for you to go after."

He suddenly thought that he should be down in Berglund taking care of business. That he was much too busy to spend any more time dawdling on the side of a mountain, looking for answers. So he said, "That sounds like a good way to look at it. Can you just give me a list of things I can do to get this all taken care of? Tell me the basics and then I'll get out of your hair."

"Hmmm." Solveig shook her head in regret. "Unfortunately, we're talking about major work that needs to be done here."

Lars tried not to take her comment personally, even though he knew deep down that she was right.

"I not only cannot give you a list of things to do to find joy," she continued. "I really would like *you* to tell *me* what things you're doing now that keep you from being satisfied."

"What are you talking about?" Lars scratched his chin.

"This is your first assignment." Solveig grinned again. "I want you to ask everyone you know what they think about you."

"That's ridiculous! I can't ask people that!" Lars quickly pictured everyone laughing at him. "The people in Berglund don't talk to each other in such a manner! Why, they're so private they never even asked my wife and me what it's like— what it *was* like—to carry Inge everywhere!"

"I know," Solveig said gently.

And Lars suddenly understood that she did know.

"But you wanted them to ask, didn't you?" she continued. "And you want them to listen to your grief at her loss. Right?"

Lars looked back out over the valley. Tears were in his eyes.

"As long as you want to learn, I will help you." Solveig took a step back from Lars. "But before you can learn, you must trust."

Lars was silent.

"Will you come back tomorrow at sunrise, and each day after?" she asked Lars. "Will you come back until you have found the way to the answers you're looking for?"

Lars tried to recall the intensity of the energy he'd felt when he'd touched Solveig. It was already fading from his body. Tentatively, he offered his promise. "If you really believe this is where I'll find what I need, yes. I'll come back."

"This is my secret meeting place," she assured him. "It has been for several decades now. I come here each day to meet with God. All He asks is that I come seeking Him. He always meets me. You will need to find your own meeting place. But this is a good place to start. I will be here and so will He." She pointed toward the peak of the mountain when she said the word "He."

Then she turned, walked away from Lars, and went through a pathway cleared in the brush. It seemed to lead around the mountain without heading up. He heard her start to sing, and he listened to that sweet, joyous song as she got farther and farther away, until all he could hear was his own heart pounding in his chest.

Lars swallowed hard and began the climb down the mountain and into the village.

F_{OUR} ❧

IT MUST HAVE BEEN a dream, Lars decided as he hiked back down. Every couple of hundred paces he would stop, shake his head, and mutter something like "I must have eaten some poisonous berry," or "Maybe I'm obsessed with not being able to save Inge," or "I have got to stop working such long hours." He made every excuse to rid himself of any responsibility to follow through on Solveig's assignment. Still, he craved more of that warm energy he'd felt when he'd touched her. Something in his heart told him not to avoid the truth he had encountered.

As he approached the village, he saw that it was still early. The familiar sounds of the new workday came as a relief to Lars. If he could only get settled into his routine at the shop, he told himself, surely his frazzled mind would return to a normal state and—

Lars stopped for a moment when he realized how long it had been since he'd craved the simplicity of everyday routine. Had his discontent with the day-to-day grind been cured by his otherworldly dream on the mountain? Perhaps he had found his answer after all. . . .

He stopped briefly at home, dropped off his backpack, hugged the boys, and promised to tell Lena about his adventure that evening.

Then he walked the path to work as he always did, but this

time there was something different. He had never noticed how the tree branches hung over the path beyond the post office . . . as if their limbs were locked in an embrace. He smiled to himself. They reminded him of the part of his dream where his hand had embraced Solveig's.

He arrived at the door to his shop and put his hand on the knob to open it, then stopped for a moment. With his hand, he traced some of the detailed carving that covered the door. Then he closed his eyes and tried to remember if the beauty of the door was new, or if he had only stopped noticing how beautiful it was.

The locksmith across the road, Sven Jorgensen, looked out through his front window and saw Lars moving his hands across his door. Although he would never dream of saying anything to Lars about this, Sven later told his wife about it over dinner.

After a few moments Lars decided that his door was indeed beautiful, even if he hadn't noticed it all these years he'd worked inside the shop. Then, by habit, he minimized the importance of his moment of appreciation. "Who looks at a silly door anyway?" he said to himself. And he began to busy himself with the tasks of the day.

He soon found that he still couldn't concentrate on work. As before, thoughts insisted on keeping his attention, and they prevented him from finishing any significant job. The only change Lars could see was which thoughts were distracting him. They were no longer angry or blaming thoughts that he was unable to shake. The words Solveig had said to him were what wouldn't leave his head. "God wants to use you to awaken the slumbering souls around you," she had said so very simply. It was as if the mountain itself were continually calling out to him.

That evening, after putting the boys to bed, Lars tried to tell his wife the details of what had happened on the mountain. She, however, said only that she wondered if he had been working too much. Maybe he should take some time off. Stay around the house.

Even though he agreed with Lena (usually the best thing to do in any situation), he could not imagine just sitting around the house. Not only was Inge's memory everywhere. He was too restless.

Settling into his bed for the first time since climbing the mountain, Lars felt fairly certain that when he woke the next morning, everything would be back to normal. But because his certainty was not complete, he felt compelled to pray.

"God, I'm not sure what You are up to, if indeed You *are* involved in this. But I need You to put everything back to normal," Lars prayed silently, staring at the ceiling above his bed. "I'm certainly open to awakening the slumbering souls around me if that is what You want me to do. But I would appreciate it if we could do it without disturbing my life too much."

He fell asleep before he could say, "Amen." And before he could feel any assurance that God had heard his prayer or that Lars' comfort was first and foremost in His mind.

In a dream, Lars again climbed the mountain. Only this time he was surrounded by dozens of other people who were desperately trying to climb as well. The other climbers kept asking Lars if he knew a shortcut to the top of the mountain. His mouth moved in response, but he was unable to say any words. He wanted to tell them that there *was* no shortcut; that you actually had to climb the whole mountain to get to the top. He helplessly watched as the other people made turns off the main trail, wandering into overgrown weeds and even off the steep, rocky edges of the mountain.

The number of climbers slowly dwindled to two, Lars and one other man whose face he did not recognize. The grief and heaviness Lars felt watching the other climbers fall off the path were so great that he felt as if his backpack were filled with stones. Lars looked at the other man with an expression that he hoped said, "You're the next one to go, and I really don't think I can bear to see one more person miss out on what is ahead."

He began to hear Solveig singing sweetly and joyfully, as she had sung when walking away from him. Lars tried to call out, "Solveig! Help us!" But still no sound came out of his mouth. "Solveig!" He fell down on his knees, but instead of landing on the path, he continued falling as if he had tumbled into an endless black pit. Arms and legs flailing, he cried one last time, "Solveig—"

Lars immediately sat up straight in his bed, sweat covering his body, his breathing heavy.

Lena rolled over and whispered, "Another bad dream, Lars? You really should . . ." She was asleep again before she finished.

A beam of moonlight broke through the window beside their bed. Lars looked down at the palms of his shaking, sweating hands, and then at their backs. A tree branch rubbed up against the window making a scratching sound, and then a tap. Another tap, then another scratch. Pause. Then two taps.

"It's a signal of some kind," Lars thought. Then the music began again, the same singing as in his dream. There was no question that it was Solveig, and that she must be near.

He jumped out of bed, pulled his boots on over his socks, and grabbed a coat to cover his nightshirt. Running outside, he immediately began whispering loudly, "Solveig! Where are you? Solveig?" He ran around the house to his bedroom window, hoping to find some sign of the old woman.

But he was alone. Only silence filled the moonlit night.

And then a faint echo of Solveig's singing drifted in on the breeze, coming from the direction of the mountain. He turned and looked at the mountain, its peak glowing.

"What kind of answered prayer is this?" Lars said to himself.

But even as he said it, a part of him knew that, truly, he was not alone. And that the question he had just asked was really meant for Someone other than himself.

FIVE ❧

THE ONLY WAY Lars could prove to himself that he had not gone completely mad, he decided, was to climb the glowing mountain again. It would soon be morning, anyway. And if he went back and didn't find the so-called meeting place, much less the old woman, he would again be free to live his life according to normal. This was what he had prayed for, wasn't it?

After leaving a note for Lena, he dressed and started out for the mountain, with no backpack this time but with great determination. He had something to prove, or rather *dis*prove. Lars' somewhat faulty logic said that if he didn't find anything remotely similar to what had happened in what he now thought of as his "two dreams," it would be enough to prove that Solveig—and God's request of him—didn't exist. He did not test this logic by, for example, asking if, when he couldn't find the keys to his shop, they had still existed or not. He clung to his cynicism as he climbed. And he tried to ignore the trace of optimism that nagged at him, insisting on the hope that he'd meet Solveig once again.

He found the path by instinct, and walked carefully along until he came to a row of bushes. They looked like the ones by the secret meeting place. Behind them was the rocky overhang.

The chirping of the birds called him to keep walking in their direction. Cautiously, he looked between the branches of the shrubs, hoping to catch a glimpse of Solveig. He could not see anything until he came to the last bush before the path opened wide. There stood Solveig's secret meeting place in all its simplicity. Everything was exactly as he had remembered it . . . except that there was no sign of the old woman.

Lars called out, "Solveig! Are you here?" He noticed how the sun was about to peek over the horizon just beyond the village below. And how the birds were singing their approval for this new day of sunshine.

His heart sank. "Well, that *is* a relief," he said, trying to convince himself. "No old woman trying to mess with my life, no unnecessary assignments. Everything is back to normal. Thank you, God!" he exclaimed, and he raised his arms to the heavens.

"Yes, thank you, God!" he heard Solveig's voice exclaim. Lars quickly turned and saw her coming around the edge of the mountain, her arms raised as well.

"I thought I would never see you again!" Lars cried out as he ran toward her.

"I *knew* I would see you again!" Solveig replied confidently, communicating the trust and confidence she had in Lars. "What I didn't know was that you'd be here before me, for a change!"

"How did you know I'd come, when I didn't even know myself?" he asked.

"Lars, you have already seen too much," she answered with a compassion in her face that calmed every nerve in Lars' body. "You cannot go back to the way you've always lived. You have wondered if there's something more, and now you know. There *is* something more. An incredible gift has already been given you. What you choose to do with it now is your gift back." Solveig looked at him gently, waiting for him to choose his answer.

He turned and looked down into the village. Seeing his house, he thought about Lena and their three—yes, *three*—children. They seemed like such gifts to him. The death of his daughter, Inge, now made this even more clear to him.

"The gift is more than your family, Lars," Solveig encouraged him, coming closer. "They will bring you more joy and love than you have ever imagined. But there is still a deeper joy and a deeper love to find."

"Solveig, you have to understand this is pretty overwhelming for me." Lars was almost pleading with her. "I spent most of yesterday thinking I was going completely crazy. I only came here to prove you're not real."

"I'll try not to take that personally," Solveig chuckled.

"No, of course it's not personal," he answered hastily. He lifted his head to watch a bird fly overhead. "But what about the dream I had last night?" Somehow he knew she already knew about his dream.

"How did you feel in that dream?" Solveig asked.

"How did I *feel*?"

"Yes," she replied simply.

"Why do you always ask such difficult questions?" Lars asked back.

Solveig smiled but said nothing.

"I felt helpless," Lars replied. "I saw people climbing this mountain, and they kept falling off. As I saw each climber fall off the path, the load I was carrying got heavier and heavier. I grew more and more angry . . . *frustrated* with the choices people were making to hurt themselves."

"Perfect!" Solveig said with one of her all-knowing glances.

Lars raised his eyebrows, questioning her response.

"That frustration, that sensitivity to the harm that can come out of the choices other people make, will carry you a long way."

"I'd like it to carry me . . . back to bed," Lars thought to himself, realizing how tired he really was.

Solveig smiled, as though reading his mind. Then she said, "So, how is your first assignment coming along?"

Lars had been afraid she would ask that question.

"I'll have to get back to you on that one," he answered evasively.

"How about tomorrow morning, then?" Solveig replied quickly.

"All right. You've convinced me. I'll do it," Lars assured her. "I'll meet you here tomorrow at sunrise."

"That's my boy," Solveig answered.

"I'm her boy?" Lars thought to himself. He found that he liked the thought. Then he saw that, clearly, Solveig had dismissed him for the day. She was already turning from him and toward the God she met here each morning. She knelt, facing away from her pupil, and became deeply quiet in a way that awed him. He watched her for a moment: She seemed lost— or was if found?—in a world he couldn't see. Lars realized there were worse things he could be than a person Solveig approved of.

After a moment or two he turned around and began walking down the path to the village. Farther down the mountain, Lars became filled with longing, for he could hear Solveig beginning to sing clearly and joyfully, just as she had sung the morning before, and just as she had sung in his dream.

Smiling, Lars decided to try to complete Solveig's assignment. For there was no other way to make the secret meeting place a place where he too would be led to such peaceful joy.

SIX ~

WHEN HE ARRIVED back in the village, Lars looked more closely at people and observed them doing things he'd never seen before. He noticed people staring at other people, watching each other intently as they went about their normal routine. Lars had always assumed no one cared what anyone else did, but perhaps this proved otherwise. This newfound perception was as fascinating to Lars as it was disturbing. For if everyone always noticed what their neighbors were doing, if they simply refrained from comment out of their definition of politeness, Lars had been remiss in ignoring their situations.

He became more aware of how mindlessly, even robotically, he could go through his day. He watched himself go through the motions of dealing with people in his shop: He would avoid eye contact with his customers and focus on the details of their requested task instead. But then, as they left the shop, a gnawing feeling would suggest that he'd missed something—could he have just as easily taken some kind of interest in that person and not only in what size nail they'd requested?

As the morning progressed, Lars decided to experiment with Solveig's assignment. He began casually asking people questions about how they perceived him.

"Good morning," he gently announced as the next customer, Karl Henie, one of the village farmers, entered his shop.

The gentleman looked at Lars and half squinted, appearing to question Lars' motives for being so friendly.

"What can I do for you today?" the hammersmith continued.

"I'm just looking for something new that I can use on my stove," Karl stated, "to cook a large serving of meat and vegetables."

"Oh, is this a gift for your wife, Karl?" Lars cautiously asked, afraid of overstepping those village-declared personal boundaries.

The man looked at Lars, his eyes opening wider, mouth gaping. "Why . . . yes, it is." He almost broke into a smile.

"Great!" Lars replied. "I know just the thing she'd like, Karl. I can have it for you by midmorning tomorrow, is that all right?"

"That would be fine." Karl turned to walk out, but Lars stopped him.

"I'm sorry, but could I just bother you with one question?"

Karl looked left and right. "Uh . . . okay," he answered, nearly choking on the words.

"What kind of reputation do I have here in the village?" Lars asked, the sweat on his brow beginning to bead up. "I mean . . . what do people say about me—you know—behind my back?"

"Um . . ." Karl cleared his throat and nervously began. "Lars? Well . . . People think that—

"This is tough. I mean, you're real great and all—" Karl took a deep breath.

"People think you are . . . nice." After he said this, he quickly turned and reached for the door.

"Thanks!" Lars called out. "Have a great day! And see you tomorrow!" As the door closed behind Karl, Lars was sure he had pushed too far.

"I am *nice*?" Lars said out loud to himself. "That's it? I've lived in Berglund my whole life, and all people think about me is that I'm nice?"

Lars knew he had a problem. Sure, he was not the village

idiot, or the village drunk—reputations that would be more difficult to mend. But . . . nice?

Not a minute had passed when the shop door opened again and in walked Tomas, a welcome and friendly sight to Lars' eyes.

"Tomas! I'm so glad to see you!" Lars boldly stated.

Tomas scratched his head. "Oh, really?"

"Yes! I sure am."

"What is the occasion?" Tomas inquired.

"No occasion. It's just—" Lars interrupted himself. "Tomas, do you think I'm nice?"

"Of course you're nice, Lars," Tomas answered, his brow wrinkled in bewilderment.

"No, I don't mean 'do you think I'm a nice person.' It's . . . Tomas, do you think that is *all* that I am? Nice, and that's all?"

"Lars, are you still on your crazy 'there has got to be something more to this life' kick?"

"No, I'm over that. I mean, I already know there *is* something more to this life," Lars attempted to explain to a still-confused Tomas. "Now I'm looking for what I'm going to do with this 'something more.' Would you mind just helping me with this one thing?"

"Sure, Lars," Tomas answered. "Yes, you are nice. But of course there's more to you than that. You are also, um . . . Well, you are . . ." He struggled to find a word, then declared, "Lars, I do not spend much time thinking about this stuff. You're kind of putting me on the spot."

"All right, Tomas. You have helped me just fine," Lars answered with a tone of resignation in his voice. It actually irritated him to think that his best friend could describe him in only such superficial terms.

Tomas looked at Lars for a minute before he said, "Lisbeth wanted me to invite you and Lena and the boys over for dinner Friday night. Could you check if that would work and let me know?"

"That sounds great. I mean, that would be *nice*." Lars

chuckled, and Tomas joined in with a smile, breaking some of the tension between them.

When Lars got home from work that evening he went right into the boys' room, where they were playing. "Hey, Jens, Erik, I have a weird question I'd like to ask you."

"Sure, Father," Jens replied while his younger brother, Erik, kept playing with his toy horse.

"What do you guys . . . um, think about me?"

Erik immediately answered, "You're the best father ever. You are strong and powerful and you like to eat a lot."

His innocence and enthusiasm made Lars smile.

"Thanks, Erik. Good answer. Jens?"

"Well . . . what exactly do you mean, Father?" Jens was the more thoughtful of the two. This was partly because he was older than Erik, and partly due to his predisposition to contemplation. He put down his book.

"I guess I'm wondering what it is you think when you think about me." Lars was trying to figure out exactly what to say while he was saying it.

"Well, Father . . . you work a lot." Jens looked up at his father and continued. "And a lot of times when I'm trying to tell you something, you seem like you're thinking about something else. Like you're not really there in your head."

Lars was stunned. "He's only eight," he thought to himself. Honesty was exactly what he had hoped to get, but he certainly hadn't thought it would contain words like these.

"That's a great answer, Jens," Lars managed to pull out as a response, even though he felt as if he'd just been hit in the face and brought to his senses. "Anything else?"

"Nah, but I'll let you know," Jens said confidently. He went back to reading his book, oblivious to the struggle stirring within his father.

"Okay. Good." Lars hesitated, not knowing quite what to say next. "I guess I'll see you at the dinner table, then." He closed the door to their room and walked toward the kitchen.

That would be where he'd find Lena.

. . .

"How was it at the shop today?" Lena asked from the cupboard, where she was choosing some potatoes. She always asked this when he arrived home.

"You know, just the same as usual," he answered, sitting down at the table.

"What happened this morning? You left so early again."

"Oh, um . . . I've decided to walk to my favorite spot on the mountain for an hour or so before dawn. Just for now, when the moon's so full." Lars hoped she wouldn't see through this half-truth. "It helps me figure things out."

Lena looked at him for moment. Then she said, "Well, thanks for the note. I would have worried without it." She carried five potatoes to the kitchen sink and intently started scrubbing them under running water, as though cleaning them were all that mattered.

"Can I bother you with a question, dear?" he finally blurted out.

"You're no bother. What is it?" she asked, and she put the cleaned potatoes in the drainboard, wiped her hands on her apron, and came over to join her husband at the table.

"I just asked the boys what they think about me."

Lena tried not to show her amusement at this comment. Or at how seriously he spoke when he told her what Jens had replied.

"So, is that true?" Lars asked, trying not to appear as desperate as he felt.

She sighed. Then she reached out her hand and, resting it on top of his, looked deep into his eyes. "I can certainly understand why he would say those things."

"But—" Lars had assumed she'd say Jens was wrong.

"And . . . I have to agree with him."

"You do?"

"Yes, I do. But please understand: I'm not mad at you for how you are. I don't think you're a bad person."

"But . . ." he said to encourage more.

She grasped his hand a bit tighter. "But I guess there's a

part in each of us that wishes things were a little different around here. You know, with you in particular."

Lars dropped his head and pulled his hand away from hers.

"Why are you asking these questions?" Lena gazed intently at her husband and continued. "You know as well as I do that life is so much easier if we stay away from questions like these."

Lars chose not to say anything about Solveig. It seemed so complicated to explain. He wanted, instead, to say that he had been thinking more about death and life and about what would need to change so that life could be more joyful for him and for the family. But when he spoke, all that came was, "I need to make up for what I didn't give Inge. But first, I need to know what I'm doing wrong."

Lena didn't respond at first. She scrubbed at a sticky spot on the table's edge. Then, almost under her breath, she said with a resentment that surprised even herself, "Since you asked, I've been wanting to talk to you since the funeral. Can't you see that we're *all* grieving in this family and it would help if you here a little more often? First your building rooms we don't need, and now these early morning walks and—"

"Lena! I'm sorry. I know I've made mistakes. But can't you see that I'm hurting here? And I'm trying to change—"

"Well, you're not the only one who's hurting!" Lena said angrily, with tears in her eyes. "And you *did* ask!"

"Yes, but I didn't expect you to be so . . . honest!" Lars couldn't think of another word.

"I guess I thought you were finally *ready* for some honesty. I see now that you're not. Just as you weren't ready for the certainty of Inge's death."

"Lena, I know you're upset about Inge's death."

"Upset?!" Her loneliness and sense of abandonment in grief, which she'd tried to contain over the past weeks, finally spilled out before she could control it. "You did nothing to help when Inge was sick. Your own daughter—and you were too busy to even pay any attention to her!" His wife pounded the table with her fist.

"Lena . . ." Lars was speechless. He'd never seen her so angry.

"Lars, I don't know what's going on inside you," she continued, "but I sure hope it means you're coming back to life. Life here. *In* this house—and not out *there* somewhere." Then she resolutely stood up from the table, and silently began plopping the potatoes into the pot already boiling on the stove.

Lars wanted to hug his wife and somehow make everything all right, but he thought Lena needed time to recover from her outburst. Words were not going to help right now, Lars thought defensively, so he said nothing.

Instead he asked himself, "Doesn't anybody really know me at all? Lena and the boys are my life. How can I make her understand that?"

He sat at the table for a while and wrestled with the gulf between his intentions and his family's experience of his actions, but he couldn't figure out how to fix it.

For the first time, Lars longed for morning, when he could bring all this to Solveig.

SEVEN ॐ

LARS AWOKE EARLY the next morning to the familiar pre-
dawn sound of birdsong. He couldn't wait to go to Solveig,
who would soon be waiting for him on the mountain. He
stretched, then looked at his still-sleeping wife beside him.
"Thank you," he whispered to her, grateful that she had let
him embrace her not long after their argument. Each had
promised to tough things out until life seemed more manage-
able. He kissed Lena on the cheek, rolled out of bed, and ran
out of the house. But as he closed the front door behind him,
he paused, remembered his boys, and went back inside and
headed for their room.

He quietly opened the door and watched them for a moment. A peace at seeing his sleeping children filled Lars, a
feeling he could not remember having had for a long time.
"All is right in the world," he thought. And then he cautiously
added, "At least for the moment." He kissed the boys on their
foreheads and left the house.

At her secret meeting place, Solveig was waiting, just as he
had expected. She greeted him by saying, "I was just praying
for you, Lars."

"Oh, really? What exactly were you praying?"

"I was praying for lots of courage and bravery," Solveig
replied.

"For me?"

"Yes, for you." She grinned that toothy grin of hers.

Lars wrinkled his brow and tried to imagine why Solveig would think he needed courage or bravery.

"She must have a new assignment for me," he finally decided. "She must already know I asked people about myself. She's skipping to the next step. I guess I won't get to ask her about Lena, after all."

"My prayer is not in preparation for a specific task or assignment you're going to face, but for a daily decision you're going to need to make—a daily decision to do what is right and true, and not just what you *feel* is the right thing."

"That doesn't sound too difficult, Solveig. I mean, can't you just tell me the right things to do and then I'll do them?" Lars didn't see why she was making this sound so difficult. "I don't like to get all wrapped up in my feelings, anyway. Feelings have never really been my strong suit."

"You make me proud when you say things like that," Solveig said.

"What *are* you talking about?" Lars was getting more and more confused by her mysterious words.

"I am going to tell you another secret," Solveig said as she leaned into his ear. Lars' eyes widened.

"Feelings have a way of controlling a person's life, more than the person can even imagine," she explained. "Your feelings tell you to do what is the most comfortable; what *appears* to be the best thing to do. If it feels right, they say, do it."

"Are you saying I have a problem with this?" Lars asked defensively.

"*Everyone* has a problem with this. It's the people who figure out how to experience the highs and lows of life *through* their feelings, without letting their feelings control them, who can most experience the love and joy we've talked about."

"I'm curious how you think I'm letting my feelings control me," Lars replied.

"First, I want to hear how it went with your first assignment!" Solveig said excitedly.

Lars was both relieved and anxious that she had asked. He was catching on to the way Solveig worked—changing subjects rather quickly, and keeping him guessing about the questions he had. Each time she did this, he was reminded that she was the one in charge of teaching him about relationship. Lars was quiet for a moment.

The only relationship Lars had ever had that even remotely resembled this one with Solveig was the one he'd had with his own father. He greatly admired his father who, when Lars was only ten, had died from some unknown disease (at least it was unknown to Lars).

His greatest memories came from times he'd spent alone with his father, watching him work in his shop or going for a walk with him on the outskirts of the village. His father had seemed gigantic to him then. Lars pictured him fondly. . . .

Lars remembered his father's shoes, covered with dirt and softened by years of wear. Then he thought about the belt his father had worn. It reminded Lars of his father's amazing gift with tools, because the buckle was intricately hammered into the picture of a canoe resting in the middle of a lake surrounded by trees. His father had said he'd made it to remind himself of a beautiful place he'd once been. Lars had always hoped to see that place someday. As a boy, he had spent hours trying to imagine what the canoe and the lake would look like in real life. . . .

Lars still had that belt, in the drawer next to his bed. He never wore it. He kept it because it was something he could touch and remember his father with, now that his father had died.

Lars thought briefly about the whiskers on his father's face. Touching those whiskers had always made him feel close to his father. . . . And his father's eyes: Lars remembered how, when he looked up at his father, those eyes told him exactly what his father was feeling: anger, joy, or, most of the time, tremendous love.

Then Lars remembered how strong his father had been

and how, even though he hadn't been extremely tall, he'd stood twice the height of his son. Yet he had never used his height or strength to intimidate or frighten Lars. Instead his father would stand as tall as he could, puff out his chest, put his hands on his hips, and proudly say, "I not only love you, Lars, but I really *like* you a lot!" Then he would crouch down to his son's level, completely envelop the boy in his arms, and hold him ever so close.

Lars had never felt more protected in his entire life.

Back on the side of the mountain, Solveig sat still while Lars reminisced, and considered how to best answer her question about how the assignment had gone. A tear began to form in his eye.

"When you're facing a difficult question, what do you think about, Lars?" she asked with incredible compassion.

"My father. He died when I was young. I think about what my father would do," Lars replied.

Solveig didn't respond, but listened intently.

"He always did the right thing. He was so strong. He always knew how to handle everything."

"And that's how you would like to be?" she gently asked.

"I'm so afraid someone is going to find out I don't know what I'm doing," Lars confessed with more anger than sorrow. "I'm afraid I'm going to make a wrong decision and something will happen to my family. Like I did with Inge. I didn't know what to do. She was only three, and crippled . . . and she died!

"Since then I feel like I'm supposed to be holding everything together . . . and I'm fooling everybody for now, but the day is coming when I'll be found out."

"Found out to be . . . what?" Solveig asked.

"I have no idea," he answered. Lars looked up into Solveig's eyes and saw that she had that *look* on her face.

She whispered gently, "Are you afraid of somebody finding out that you need help getting through this little adventure called life? Of seeing you as you really are?"

Lars looked up to the sky, and a tear spilled onto his cheek. A bird flew over their heads, singing its beautiful song as if everything were perfect in the world.

"Will you help me, Solveig? I need you to help me," Lars confessed.

"Yes, Lars," she responded. "*We* will help you." Solveig pointed to the top of the mountain and smiled. It was not necessarily a smile of happiness, but rather a smile of relief.

Lars breathed in deeply, let out a huge sigh, and closed his eyes.

EIGHT ⤮

LARS AND SOLVEIG sat down against the side of the mountain. This provided the best view of the sun rising over the village as it brought trees and houses to life with its light. He began to tell Solveig everything he had learned about himself from the first assignment.

"What surprised you most about their responses?" Solveig wondered.

"It surprised me that my best friend, Tomas, could not say anything more about me than he did. It did *not* surprise me, as much as I wish it would have, to hear my oldest boy, Jens, tell me how I never appear to listen to what he says." He paused. "But I guess I was most surprised by my wife, Lena."

"Why?"

"She lost her temper, and shouted about what she and the boys need from me. She didn't seem to even notice that I'm trying to—"

"What did you expect her to say?"

Lars took a moment to think about it. "I have no idea," he admitted, and lapsed into silence again.

Solveig watched him expectantly.

Finally he said, "I wish she would have told me things were bothering her sooner, instead of keeping everything inside and then throwing it at me all at once."

"My intuition tells me," Solveig said in a teasing tone, "that you need to let go of *that* wish as soon as possible."

Lars tried to defend himself. "But if she would just tell me exactly what she and the boys need from me, I'd be glad to change!"

"For some reason, Lena doesn't believe that. Or else she would already have told you," Solveig added.

Lars was silent a moment. "I suppose you're going to tell me you agree with her?" he asked ruefully. He sighed. "And I suppose you'd both be right."

Solveig smiled. "Lars, God has made you with certain qualities. And along the way, through a series of choices you have made, you've become who you are. You are not an accident. In the same way, you now have a chance to decide who you want to become." She continued, "It is your turn to take charge of the person you are, the person other people see. With a little work, it will be the same person!" Solveig chuckled.

Lars wanted to be able to chuckle along with her, but all he could manage was a tiny smile. "Solveig, sometimes you make my head spin," he confessed.

"Remember when I told you that whoever dares to step out in faith will be met with help?"

"Yes . . ." Lars answered.

"You are doing that. The mountain you're climbing is larger than the piece of rock we're standing on. You are climbing a path most people never even try . . . because it is so difficult." Solveig continued, "It is now time to receive the help you need."

Lars looked around, thinking Solveig was about to give him a backpack full of tools and supplies. Or a collection of manuals or books on how to climb would help.

Instead Solveig held out her hands to Lars. "Open your hands," she said.

"Both of them?"

"Yes," Solveig replied with a serious look on her face, as if she were beginning some kind of ceremony. Lars held out his open hands.

She began, "Lars, I have told you several secrets. This is one I want you to tell to everyone you can, but only after you truly understand what it means for yourself."

His hands began to shake slightly. Lars looked down at them and hoped Solveig would not see. She reached out and took hold of his hands. Again he felt that reassuring warmth of Love at her touch.

"I have told you that the secret to the life you're looking for is found in letting go," Solveig said calmly. "And in balancing reason and emotion. And that God made no mistake when He made you as you are—even when that means you need others to get things done."

Lars nodded in agreement.

"These open hands represent your admitted need for help. So many people try to fill their hands with all kinds of things —things that look important or valuable—so that they never have to see how empty their hands really are. Whenever you look down at your empty hands, remember this: On your own, you have nothing."

Solveig reached into her pocket and pulled out a beautiful ring. It was a solid band of gold that reflected the rising sun as she held it high above her head.

"This ring is to remind you always that you are never alone." She placed the gold band in his hand. "Keep this in your pocket. Whenever you need help climbing whatever mountain you're facing, or even when you're resting in the valley, you can touch the ring and know that you are not alone. But remember, don't show it to anyone, not even to Lena . . . especially not to Lena. She might misunderstand; she also could feel left out, and God doesn't want anyone to feel resentful or left out. This ring is something between you and Him."

"Solveig . . ." Lars did not know what to say. Solveig put her finger up to her lips, silencing him for the moment.

"We have our secret meeting place here, and God is with us," she continued. "But when you come down off the mountain, God is still with you, longing for you to be in a relationship with Him—a relationship that will allow you to meet

Him in your own secret meeting place, and there find the wisdom and inspiration to live the life you are looking for."

"What do you mean by 'having a relationship' with God?" Lars was trying as best he could to understand everything Solveig had to tell him.

"As with any relationship—the one you have with Lena included—it is important to communicate," Solveig explained. God wants to know your thoughts and your feelings, and He wants you to know His. You will begin to understand more about yourself by what God says to you, rather than by what you feel. Your entire life will be different. His wise heart can change your character and thinking."

Lars couldn't help but ask naively, "Does this mean I have to go to church every day?"

Solveig laughed. "No. You do not have to go to church to meet with God. He is with you wherever you go. This ring is to remind you of that."

Lars looked confused.

"It's okay if you don't understand all this right now," she reassured him. "It's a process. Your understanding will deepen for the rest of your life . . . if you let it."

Understanding. Lars thought about his father, who had always understood him. What would he have thought about this mountainside scene? Lars pictured himself in his father's embrace, remembered how he had felt when surrounded by his father's arms. Loved. Protected. And strong. Feeling his father's strength had made him feel strong even as a young boy. Now, as a grown man, recognizing his failures as a husband and a father had led him to a source of strength and comfort he'd never known to be available to him.

"My father—" Lars said aloud, then he choked up and could not finish his thought.

Solveig added, "—would have been very proud of you."

Slipping his hand in his pocket, he felt the new ring there. For the first time since he was ten, Lars knew that he was loved completely.

NINE

LARS PICTURED LENA'S smiling face and warm embrace after he told her about this new love he had found—or rather, received.

"I'd better get home to my wife," he said to Solveig. "I'm going to help her get the boys ready for school." Then he stopped, felt the ring, and added with a tone of surprise, "I've never said those words in my life!"

Solveig smiled.

"Before I leave, do you have an assignment for me?" Lars asked somewhat hesitantly.

She thought for a moment. There was so much she wanted to say. "I want you to think about what kind of relationship you want to have with God."

"Do you mean *I* get to decide?" Lars could not believe his ears.

"Everybody gets to decide what kind of relationship they're going to have with God. That's the beautiful part." Solveig grinned as she laid out his options. "God seldom imposes Himself on anyone. He stands at the door of your life and knocks. You can open the door and invite Him in to stay— often or just on occasion. Or you can simply never answer the knock."

"So, I'm the one in control?" he asked.

"Well . . ." she hesitated. "Yes, you are. It's much like a

person standing on the shore of the ocean. The waters are deeper than any mere human could manage. Still, the water calls that person to jump in and swim as much as he desires. It never insists either that the man jump in or how far he should go. It simply offers its water."

"I'm not much of a swimmer," Lars said with a smile. "You want me to figure out how far I want to swim?" he asked her.

"You can get just your feet wet, or you can dive in and get completely lost in the flow of the water," Solveig replied.

Lars had thought he understood, but the more she talked about it, the more confused he felt. "I'm sorry, Solveig, but can you translate this into simpler words for me?"

"Of course, Lars," she assured him. "In any relationship, you have the opportunity to spend as much time as you desire with the other person. You can decide how much you tell the other person about your life. You also get to decide what influence you're going to allow the other person to have on you. It's the same with God."

"But I can't see Him!" Lars responded.

"Yes, but you can see your ring, correct?"

"Of course."

"Just as that ring is close to you when you carry it, God is always with you," Solveig explained. "Of course, you can lose your ring. And you can ignore God. But unlike a forgotten or lost ring, neither you, nor anything else, will ever be able to separate you from the love God has for you."

"Do you mean there is nothing I can do to make God stop loving me?" he said in a wondering tone.

"God will never stop loving you, no matter what you do, even if you sometimes feel or act as if He has," she told him. "But that gets us back to the whole issue of not letting only your feelings tell you what the truth is, or how you should behave."

"Thank you, Solveig," Lars told her, looking down at the ring. "Your gift is more beautiful and more meaningful than I could ever have dreamed."

"The gift I've given you is not something that's been

placed in your hand. It's something that has been placed in your heart." Solveig looked him in the eyes and continued, "They can cut off your hand, or even your whole arm. They can take away your family, or anyone or anything that means a lot to you. But no one can ever take away what is in your heart."

"Solveig, please don't ever leave," Lars pleaded as he moved toward her and hugged her tightly. It was the first time he had ever tried to embrace her.

"I must go," she said, pulling away. "And you must return to the village. Your life is with your family and your friends. I will see you again, Lars."

"Solveig . . ."

She again placed her finger up to her lips to silence him, turned around, and began the walk down her usual path that led around the mountain. The sound of her singing drifted up to Lars on the morning breeze.

Awestruck, Lars was now certain that Solveig must be an angel.

TEN ✦

ON HIS WALK BACK DOWN the mountain, Lars still couldn't wait to see Lena and the boys. He hoped to arrive home before Jens and Erik left for school, because he sensed a change taking place in his life.

He paused in the middle of the path, looked up to the sky, and prayed, "God, I'm not exactly sure what You're doing, but I like it. I feel like I can enjoy life more. I can love the people around me more. I can even enjoy being by myself more than I ever could before. Please feel free to keep doing whatever it is You're doing."

Lars wondered if being so casual with God was disrespectful. But then he smiled. Solveig had told him that God just wanted to know what he was feeling. And feelings were not formal things.

So he continued, "And God, please don't let me ever get so 'religious' that I know all the right words to say! Amen."

When he arrived home, Lars stopped in front of the kitchen window and caught a glimpse of his boys and his wife sitting at the table. Moving to the side so they wouldn't see him, he watched them eat their breakfast together. The boys were talking with their mother. Although he couldn't hear what they were saying, Lars could see how they enjoyed laughing with her. "They look so happy," he thought. He watched how Lena affectionately ran her hand through Jens' hair, and how he smiled up at her in return. Then she hurried the boys away from the table to get them ready to leave.

Lars entered through the front door, just in time to catch the boys running toward their room.

"Father!" they both shouted, and they turned and lunged forward to hug Lars.

"I do love you two children," he replied in response to their affection.

"Me too, Father," Jens answered softly.

"Me *too* . . . too, Father!" Erik shouted.

"Are you ready for school?" Lars asked them.

"Yes, sir!" they answered, and ran off to their room for their books and jackets.

Lena approached Lars in the front hallway. "They're excited to see you," she said, looking deep into Lars' face.

"Yes, where do you think that came from?"

"There's something different in your eyes, Lars," she responded. "Something that especially a child can see." She paused, and then asked, "What's going on in you, Lars?"

"Only good, Lena," he answered as the boys ran back to their parents by the front door. "Have a great day at school today, okay?" their father told them.

"Yes, sir," they replied.

"And if you get in trouble, try to make it look like it was the other person's fault."

"Lars!" Lena exclaimed.

"Yes, sir," they again said in unison. Then they hugged Lars and Lena, and ran out the front door.

"Would you like a cup of coffee?" Lena asked, hoping she might get her husband to talk with her a bit.

"I'd love some coffee," he replied as they walked into the kitchen.

Lena remained quiet, to see if Lars would begin the conversation. Since their argument, she had hoped he'd figure out how to set things right.

"Lena, do you believe in God?" he asked, looking up at his wife, thinking this would be a safe place to start.

"Of course, Lars. Doesn't everybody?" she answered as she poured the coffee.

"But you, Lena, do *you* believe in God?" he continued.

"Lars, what is your point?" This seemed to be starting off the way their talk the other day had. They never talked about this sort of thing.

"What I'm trying to ask is, what kind of relationship do you have with God?"

"I wonder if that is actually possible, Lars," she said tentatively. "It seems to me that having a relationship with someone implies that they actually care about you. I cannot help but wonder if God really cares about us. What about Inge? . . . Wouldn't she still be alive if He cared for us?"

"Lena, you asked what's going on with me. *This* is what is going on with me. I've been walking and thinking—" Lars said, trying to stay calm. "I'm starting to believe God wants us to feel His love—no matter what happens to us. So, when bad things or good things happen, He is there to help us and to love us."

"I'm not so sure about that," Lena replied. "I just know it's probably best to get on His good side. And that is what I hope to be able to do."

"But why, Lena?" he asked strongly. "There must be something inside you telling you to do that!"

"I guess it's just . . . a hope that it will protect the rest of us from more bad things."

Lars tried not to lose his temper. He was frustrated that his wife seemed so unaware of what he had so recently learned about God—the real God, not the one-dimensional God he'd heard preached so often. And he was frustrated that he, Lars, couldn't come up with the right words to help her understand what he now *knew* in so deep a way.

Lars felt for his ring, took a deep breath, and tried a new approach—one of humility. "Lena, I love you so much. I'm so sorry for everything I've done that has kept me at a distance from you. I've been very busy, by my own choosing. And my relationship with you and the boys has suffered." He swallowed deeply and looked Lena intently in the eyes. "You are a wonderful wife. I could not ask for anything more from you. Please forgive me for not seeing that as much as I could have."

Lena was stunned by what Lars was saying. She walked over to him and felt his forehead. "Hmm, no fever," she said, chuckling a little.

Lars grabbed her hand and pulled her into a light embrace. Startled, she automatically wrapped her arms around him, and they stood together, arms entwined. Lars held Lena delicately, as if she were made of china. Then he took her face into his hands and drew it so close to his own face that she felt his breath, and smelled the coffee they just shared. He looked at every part of her face. Her eyes—though they were beginning to show signs of age around the corners, they were of the same blue that he had fallen in love with more than fifteen years ago in high school. Her nose softly drew his eyes down her face to her lips, which were just plump enough to invite a kiss. Lars ran his thumbs across her upper lip first, starting in the center and moving outward; then the bottom lip. He felt a slight quiver in her lips as he touched them.

He could have kissed her at this point, but instead he spoke softly to her. "Lena, I'm finished loving you the way I have been. If you'll let me, I have a new love to give you." Lars knew the words he was speaking were not his own. He continued, "It is a love that goes beyond what even I can understand. It's a love that says I'll never leave you. It says I'm no longer the most important thing in my life. It also means I'm willing to give more of me to you than I ever imagined possible. This is the love I want to give you."

They kissed as they had not kissed since their children were born.

"Of course, only if *you* are interested," he added.

"Yes, Lars, I am. I am *very* interested," Lena replied.

"That's a relief!" They laughed together and held their embrace just a little bit tighter.

ELEVEN ✐

LARS KNEW THIS WAS going to be a good day. As he walked
to his shop to begin his day's work, he could not help but
thank God for his time with Lena that morning. He wasn't exactly sure how their time together had become such a success—their conversation about God hadn't been particularly
profound; the coffee had been its usual aromatic but not perfect brew. Something had happened, though, when he'd apol-
ogized to Lena. Had that made the difference? It was as if
saying "I'm sorry" was what he'd needed to free himself, to be
able to understand how much he loved Lena, and to be able to
tell her that convincingly.

He decided that they should make coffee drinking a regu-
lar part of their day-to-day routine. He was sure Lena would
agree. So, during some of his free time in the shop, Lars made a
couple of special cups for them to use each morning.

Now and then throughout the day, Lars reached into his
pocket to touch the new ring while he was working. He would
stop what he was doing and take a moment to try talking with
God.

"God," he began, "I don't know quite what to say to You.
But 'thanks' seems to be a good place to start." He looked
around for things to say thanks for. "Thanks for Solveig.
Thanks for giving me this shop. Sure, it was handed down
through the years, and many times I thought it was actually a

curse, rather than a blessing. . . . But it has been really good for me to have this place to come each day and use my hands to make things for other people." Lars felt a little silly at the things he was saying, but he figured it would get easier to say things to God as time went by.

"Thanks for Lena and her incredible heart. Thanks for giving her patience to be able to put up with me. Thanks for Inge—" He stopped for a moment, missing his daughter tremendously. Then he thought about his two living boys, and about the gift of love his own father had given him. "God, thank you for my father. And for Jens and Erik. Please protect them today. Help me to be the kind of father they need. I want to show them how much I love them—something I know I'm going to need Your help to do."

Lars closed his eyes. For the first time he pictured Jens as a man, talking to his own son about *his* father. He heard him tell his son how his father had never listened to him, always seeming to be somewhere else.

"My father tried really hard to be good man, but he wasn't able to figure out how to be the kind of father I needed," Lars imagined his son saying. "I just wanted to know he'd be there for me, not only when I needed him, but even when I just wanted to be with him."

Stunned by his vivid daydream, Lars opened his eyes and saw his workbench, as always, covered with many sizes of hammers and scraps of metal. He picked up the piece he was working on, chose the right size hammer, and began working again.

If anger and frustration were the seeds out of which determination grew, Lars figured, he could be thankful for even those emotions. He resolved not to let his daydream about Jens turn into reality.

The door to his shop opened, and in walked Karl Henie.

"Good morning, Karl!" Lars said in greeting.

"Hello, Lars."

"I have your new pot all ready for you. I even wrapped it nicely for when you give it to your wife."

Karl murmured, "Thank you so much, Lars. I—"

Lars put his finger up to his mouth to silence Karl. "You don't have to say anything. It was my pleasure."

"Do you mind if I sit down for a minute?" Karl asked as he pulled up a chair to Lars' workbench.

"Of course not, Karl. What's going on?"

"Oh, not a whole lot," he answered sheepishly, as if something actually *was* going on.

Lars sat in silent amazement at how little it took to encourage even a Berglunder to open up.

"That's not completely true, Lars," Karl confessed. "Remember how you asked me the question about how you come across to people?"

"Of course I do."

"Well, Lars, I haven't been able to stop thinking about that."

Lars asked hopefully, "You have a better answer for me today?"

"To be honest, I haven't been thinking about you at all. But I *have* been thinking about *me*."

Lars smiled as Karl continued. "It's been driving me crazy because I don't think people could say that *I* am nice. I don't think people know me at all. That doesn't seem right to me."

Lars thought this might be a good time to take another chance with Karl. "Let me ask you this, Karl. Have you ever talked to God about this?"

Karl looked puzzled.

"It's just a thought," Lars added.

"You know I see you every Sunday at church, Lars," Karl began. "But you've changed. . . . Do you think God is personally interested in me, at all? Do you think God really cares about how I come across to other people?"

"Yes, I believe He is, and He does," Lars said in an assured tone that surprised even himself.

"How, Lars?" Karl asked.

"Well, I don't know exactly how, or why, but I know He does. I know God wants to know what's going on inside you

—your thoughts and feelings—and He wants you to know His. It's very similar to the relationship you have with your wife."

This kind of talking was foreign to Karl. Still, he was desperate enough to be curious about what Lars was trying to tell him. "What is God going to do about changing the way I come across to people?" he asked Lars.

"I cannot answer that for you—only God knows what He's going to do in your life. But if you let Him, He *will* change you. I'm certain of that."

"Thanks for your interesting thoughts, Lars," Karl said, and he started toward the shop door.

"Karl, I didn't really answer your question. But perhaps you can think about another question that might need to be answered first."

"What is that?" Karl asked as he turned back toward Lars.

"Karl, what kind of relationship do you *want* to have with God?"

"That's a very good question, Lars. But for now, I really have to get home." Karl was obviously uncomfortable. "Oh, and thanks for the new pot." Karl turned back to the door and hurried out.

The door closed behind him, leaving Lars alone once again. "You are welcome," he said to himself.

This was the second person Lars had questioned about his or her desire for God. First Lena. Now Karl. He wasn't so much on a mission to get everybody thinking about God as he was interested in completing Solveig's assignments and processing his own thoughts about Him.

Lars wasn't sure if what he had just done was a good thing or a bad thing.

"God, I'm not sure what happened here," Lars began to pray. "But I do ask that You will show Yourself to Karl and let him know how much You love him. Help him see how much more important it is to know what *You* think about him, than it is to worry about what other people think about him."

Lars stopped praying when he heard the last words he had

said. He was surprised by how profound they were. And he wondered if that idea was something Solveig had said, or if he had come up with it on his own.

It didn't matter so much who had come up with the words, he finally decided. Lars knew he had needed to hear them either way.

*T*WELVE

THROUGHOUT THE REMAINDER of the day in his shop, Lars' thoughts turned back to his son, Jens. His determination to make a positive impact on him as a father and a friend continued to grow. Lars desperately needed to know how to relate to his boys. Because he was beginning to get used to the idea of telling God what he was thinking, Lars prayed out loud. His words were filled with urgency, for he wanted to solve this problem immediately.

"God, you know how much I love my boys," Lars began. "And while I haven't been the greatest at showing them exactly how I feel about them, I think now is a really good time for me to make some changes in how I treat them. But I need Your help—because I have no idea what I'm supposed to do."

Even though his eyes were open the entire time he was talking, when he finished, he looked around the room to see if anything was different. It was completely silent. Nothing had changed. He certainly didn't feel as though God had revealed anything to him about how to deal with his boys, and he wondered if He ever would. Lars sat in the silence for a short while—hoping for a signal of some kind that would prove God was listening.

"I'm going to trust that You are in control," Lars finally said to finish his prayer. "And that, even when You don't give me an answer when I want it, You are going to lead me toward Your answer."

Lars immediately felt a release of the tension that had been building up inside him. He didn't have any answers yet, but he felt calm and peaceful, and somehow he knew that everything was going to work out. This faith of his was so new to Lars that he didn't know what to call it. He just knew that he had it, probably for the first time ever.

At dinner that evening, Lena and Lars sat in their usual places across the table from the two boys. But tonight it was *two* parents who enjoyed being with their children as they ate and discussed the activities of the day. Even when the boys spoke only about the games they had made up on the playground after school, Lars and Lena paid full attention, basking in all that excitement for life that shone in the eyes of their boys.

"And then . . . um . . ." Erik was describing in detail what his friend had done to a girl on the playground. "Um . . . Soren went up to her . . ." He took a bite of his food and continued, "and he rumpled it wif a hap an roobied it to da harg." Erik swallowed the food that was in his mouth. "Can you believe it? It's true! I was there!"

Lars smiled at his wife and then said enthusiastically to his youngest son, "Erik! That's unbelievable!"

"I know!" Erik replied.

"Jens, how about you, son?" Lars asked. "How was your day?"

"Fine," he answered, keeping his head lowered and his eyes on his food.

Lars looked to Lena, raising his eyebrows as if to ask her, "Did something bad happen to him?" She responded by shrugging her shoulders—she didn't know of anything.

"What did you do today?" Lars asked.

Jens looked up at his father with a face that showed both sadness and confusion. With courage he asked, "Why do you climb the mountain, Father?"

"What are you talking about, Jens?" Lars had no idea his son, or anyone other than Lena and Solveig, for that matter, knew about his trips up the mountain.

"Father, they were talking about you on the playground today—about how you climb the mountain. They all said you're crazy to do that."

Sensing that Jens had more to say, Lars waited. As he waited, he tried to imagine who could have seen him head up the mountain these last few days.

"They said everyone who climbs the mountain never comes back . . . because they die. I don't want you to die, Father!" Jens began to cry.

Lars got up from his seat, moved to the other side of the table, and held his son in his arms. "I'm not going to die, Jens."

Lena set down her fork; Erik continued eating.

"Is it true, Father? Is it true?" Jens asked.

Lars pulled his chair around the table to sit down next to his son. "Yes, Jens, it is true that I climb the mountain." Lars looked over at Lena and saw the "I told you so" look on her face. He was sure she was getting ready to demand that they return to the old, safe ways so that no negative comments would be aimed at their sons. "But it is a *good* thing," Lars continued.

"Really, Father? How is it a good thing?" Jens questioned his father.

Lars now spoke as much to Lena as he did to Jens. "Son, I'm at a place in my life where I'm trying to figure out how to be the best father, the best husband, the best *man*, I can be," he explained. "Climbing the mountain is a great help for me— and I need a lot of help!"

Lena couldn't help but ask, "How is climbing a silly mountain helping you with all this?"

Lars took a deep breath and sat up straighter in his chair. "I have made a friend on the mountain—someone who knows a lot more about this life than I could ever know."

"Is this 'friend' a man or a woman?" Lena asked in a steely undertone.

Lars understood what his wife was thinking. She had never been a jealous person—she'd had no reason to be. But with Lars' recent behavior—slipping out of the house in the middle of the night, and even appearing to be happier than usual—he was sure she was beginning to wonder what was going on with her husband.

"Her name is Solveig."

"Oh, Lars." Lena dropped her head in her hands.

"And she's probably eighty years old."

Lena still had her face in her hands, but she began to laugh out loud. "Eighty?" she asked through her laughter. "Eight-zero?"

"Yes, eighty," Lars replied. "What is so funny?"

"Nothing," Lena forced out while Lars shot her a look of confusion across the table.

"Do we get to meet her?" Erik asked enthusiastically.

"Yeah, when do we get to meet this 'friend' of yours?" Lena added.

"Well, I'm not sure when. But it would be great if you could," Lars answered. "I was going to ask Jens if he'd be interested in going up the mountain with me tomorrow morning."

"Do you really mean that, Father?" Jens said eagerly, his face brightening.

"Of course I do, son. But we'll have to leave pretty early to make it up the mountain and back before you have to be at school."

"That'll be great! I'll go to bed right now!" Jens got up and began to run from the table.

"Jens," Lars said sternly, causing his son to stop in his tracks and turn toward his father.

"I'm sorry, Father. May I be excused?"

"Yes, you may." Jens ran off, with his little brother following close behind him. "You too, Erik."

"Honey, he's only eight. Are you sure it's safe?" Lena could not help but be concerned about her son.

"Yes, he'll be fine. I'll be right there to help him along the entire way. And between you and me," he continued, moving closer to Lena, "it's not too far up the mountain. And I found a trail that's not too difficult."

"Maybe it's not too difficult for a grown man, but for an eight-year-old, Lars?"

"Trust me, Lena."

"Trust you with the life of my son?"

"He's *our* son, Lena. And yes, you can trust me," Lars assured her.

Still hesitant to give her approval on the next morning's climb, Lena sighed. It was clear that she was struggling against her need to protect her son against rash decisions her husband might make and her desire to respect her husband, who was obviously being led somewhere new to them both. She nodded almost imperceptibly, stood up, and left the room. Though she had not spoken, Lars felt in her a fragile willingness to trust her growing awareness that change was not always a bad thing.

Alone in the kitchen, Lars touched his ring and prayed silently, "God, she needs to trust me, and I need to trust You. Please help me, and please help Lena know everything is going to be all right."

Lars didn't get the same peaceful feeling he'd had after his earlier prayer that day. Instead he felt very anxious. Was Lena right? Was taking Jens up the mountain a foolish, unnecessary risk? Or was this leading he'd received right: this nagging feeling that the risk was worth what could come out of the trip with his son?

Getting any sleep that night was going to be a challenge.

THIRTEEN

FOR JENS, MORNING CAME faster than it ever had before. It seemed as if he'd barely put his head on his pillow, when he opened his eyes and saw Lars leaning over his bed, kissing him awake. On a normal school day, Jens usually took his time getting up. But today was different. He jumped out of bed, startling his father, not only with his quickness, but also with the obvious fact that Jens had slept in his clothes.

"Come on, Father! Hurry up!" Jens exclaimed as he ran out of his room, leaving Lars still standing by his son's bed. The boy ran to the front entryway of the house and began putting on his shoes.

Lena hadn't awakened for her husband's other morning climbs, but she wanted to make sure she saw the two of them out the door today. She still appeared a bit nervous about their hike as she handed Lars a backpack filled with food she had prepared for them. Lars was anxious too, but he figured it best to not say anything to Lena about it.

"You don't have to tell us to be careful, Mother," Jens confidently stated. "I'll take care of Father. He'll be just fine." Lars and Lena smiled at each other.

Lars added, "And I promise, if something horrible happens to Jens, I'll drag him all the way down the mountain by his toenails."

Jens' eyes widened.

Lars winked at his son and ended with, "So we don't clutter up the mountain with his body."

"Not funny, Lars," Lena responded.

"No, Father, that wasn't very funny at all," Jens added with a look of disgust.

Lars tried defending himself. "I was teasing! I promise!"

"Please don't let Jens be late for school," Lena asked of Lars.

"No worries," Lars assured her. "We'll just go up the mountain, talk to Solveig for a couple of minutes, and be back before you can say 'poison ivy.' "

"Okay, Father. I'm ready to go!" Jens was growing impatient.

Lena bent down to kiss Jens on the forehead. Then she tipped his head up to kiss him on the lips as well. She hugged him tightly.

"Lena," Lars began, "we *will* be back. I promise."

She kissed Lars, and then watched them walk into the darkness of the early morning.

The sun had not yet officially risen when Lars and Jens began their hike up the mountain. The sky had a faint glow that served as a gentle sign that the sun was on its way over the horizon.

"This is pretty easy, Father," Jens said, referring to their climbing of the mountain, even though they had barely reached the point where the path started to get steep.

"It sure is a lot easier having you here with me!" Lars told his son in a tone more confident than he really felt. "But I have to tell you, Jens, while it may be easy now, it's going to get a lot more difficult pretty soon."

"Oh, Father. You'll be fine." Jens responded.

"Thanks. You know, I really needed to hear that!"

"And don't worry about me. I have really strong legs."

"That's a good thing, Jens." Lars smiled at his son.

As the climb got more difficult Lars wrestled with his thoughts. Would it be better to put his son in front of him so that he could protect him from the back? Or to lead the way himself, testing the rocks and the pathway for his son trailing in the rear? He decided to follow his son, so that he could keep an eye on his every move. Still, Lars followed close enough to be able to catch the boy if he were to trip or fall.

Climbing over large rocks and avoiding fallen tree limbs on the increasingly steep trail, young Jens started to breathe heavily. "Father . . . um . . . why . . ." He paused to catch his breath, then tried again. "Why . . . do you . . . climb . . . the . . . mountain?"

Lars stopped their climb for a minute and allowed his son to catch his breath. "Sometimes it gets very hard to keep doing things the same way all the time," Lars tried to explain. "It seems to me that everybody in Berglund wants to keep doing things the way they've always done them. But I don't. Especially since your sister died."

"Mom says Inge is happy in heaven. And that Erik and I are probably going to be here on Earth for a long time, till we're old."

Lars stopped, grateful beyond words that Lena had been tending to the boys' grief while he, Lars, had been oblivious to their need. He talked with Jens for a little, about Inge and how she had found a way to love life, despite its hardships. And then Lars said, "I have this hunger inside my heart that tells me to look for more in life—"

"I'm starting to feel a little hungry myself," Jens said, and he rubbed his stomach. They found a rock to sit on and opened the backpack to see what food Lena had packed for them.

Lars handed Jens a sandwich, but did not eat much himself. Still on edge about how this journey would come out, he didn't have much appetite.

"What I've found is that the change I'm looking for is actually inside me, rather than in anything or anybody around me." Lars was trying his best to explain his situation in a way his eight-year-old son could understand. Contentedly eating his sandwich, Jens did appear to catch at least a little of what his father was saying.

"And what is happening," Lars continued, "is that I'm learning more about what it means to be a good father to you and Erik, and a good husband to your mother."

Lars looked at his son and so desperately wanted to tell him about the daydream he'd had, and how he was determined to not let it become reality. He wanted to find just the right words to tell him about all the things he was learning in his heart—about how he was beginning to understand that God wanted to have a relationship with him. . . .

Then he thought about his own father and the walks they had taken together. Lars couldn't remember many specific things that his father had said to him during their time together. Instead, what he clearly remembered was the feeling of being best buddies with him—the feeling that his father thought the world of him and that he would do anything in his power to make his son happy. Those memories relieved Lars, and reminded him that all he had to do was simply enjoy spending time with Jens.

"Son, I want you to know how much I love you," Lars said to his son. "There's nothing you could do that would ever change that. Nothing you can do will make me love you less, and nothing you do will make me love you more."

He found that he was finally able to hold eye contact with his son while he said these words. Lars was just telling himself that this was truly a moment that his son would remember for years and years to come, when Jens suddenly said, "I have to go to the bathroom." The boy slid off the rock they were sitting on, slipped behind a bush, and then returned to declare, "Come on, Father. Let's go!"

Lars gathered up the food they had laid out on the rock, put it all back in the backpack, and slipped off the rock and onto the trail.

Lars laughed out loud at the innocence of his son, at his desire to grab hold of every moment with great enthusiasm. Jens seemed at peace with everything that had happened in the past, not at all concerned about what was going to happen in the future.

"When did I lose that?" Lars thought to himself. He began to think about God and wondered if He had suggested this trip with his son more for him, Lars, than for Jens. "God, are you trying to tell me something here?" Lars asked. "Are you telling me it's time to stop worrying about all I need to be in the future? And to be more grateful for what I have already become?"

Lars thought this would have been a great time for some of those birds that usually flew overhead to show up—they always seemed to be a sort of sign affirming his spiritual wondering.

No such luck. All he heard was the crackling of twigs and leaves beneath their feet while they walked the mountain path. He looked up and saw the shadow of overhead branches against the increasingly blue sky.

For patience, Lars held on to the ring from Solveig. He slipped it on his finger momentarily and held his hand before him. By doing so, he covered up his view of his son. So he spread his fingers apart, looked through them, and watched Jens walking ahead of him. He opened and closed his fingers a couple of times, changing the perspective each time he opened them. Even with his fingers opened, Lars could keep his eyes on his hand, making Jens seem out of focus. He slipped the ring back in his pocket.

"God," Lars began, "please help keep my eyes focused on what You want me to see, and not just on what *I* want to look at."

With that, continuing in faith seemed just barely possible. Lars felt much more comfortable, though, with the more familiar thought that followed: They could turn around and head back home, where Jens would certainly be safe. So Lars touched his ring one more time, took a deep breath, and said sternly to himself, "Solveig will be waiting." And they continued on.

FOURTEEN ৵

LARS AND HIS BOY were nearly halfway to the meeting place when Jens cried out, "Father, look at this!" and ran off into the rough weeds on the right side of the path. Lars felt his heart skip a beat when he saw his son run off the trail. Obviously, something had caught Jens' eye, but Lars couldn't see what it was. Jens had run off so quickly that Lars actually had to work to keep up with him.

If Lars had stopped to think for a minute, he probably would have demanded that Jens quit running, since they were possibly heading into dangerous territory. But it was as if Jens' naive thirst for the unknown had taken over his father as well, compelling Lars to find what it was his son had seen. He called out to Jens, but all he heard in reply was the wind in his ears as he ran after him.

Jens continued running downhill for what felt to Lars like five minutes. "Surely his vision is not *that* good," Lars wondered. As his breathing became heavier and each step more and more challenging, it appeared as if his son were actually moving in slow motion—running and jumping over small obstacles, his hair bouncing up and down.

And then, just as Lars was an arm's length from his son, he reached out and tried to grab the boy. His son, though, jumped up, onto a giant fallen tree, and then he disappeared over its edge.

Lars froze in his tracks and gasped as his stomach lurched into his throat. He could see nothing now but blue sky beyond the fallen tree. Surrounded by silence, he was consumed for just a moment with immense fear.

Then, desperate to reach his son, Lars instinctively ran after him. He reached the fallen tree and pulled himself onto it. He was nearly out of breath from running, and what he saw from the tree trunk completely took away any breath that remained.

It was the most glorious sight Lars had ever seen!

Jens had landed in the largest field of wild daisies that Lars could ever have imagined. The field seemed endless, and Jens was already about fifty yards away, leaping through it with wild abandon.

"Come on, Father! Isn't it great?" Jens called out.

"Wait for me!" Lars responded. He jumped off the tree and ran to join his son in the field of flowers.

When he finally caught up with Jens, Lars grabbed his son's hands and began swinging him around in a circle.

"Faster, Father, faster!" Jens cried out.

Lars actually spun him so fast that Jens' legs rose up off the ground and started to swing outward. The boy's feet cleared the tops of all the flowers, occasionally skimming one or two with his toes.

Jens closed his eyes and held his mouth wide open as he was swung around. "I'm flying, Father! I'm flying!" he shouted.

"Yes, you are!" Lars answered.

Jens opened his eyes and looked straight at Lars—they were both getting dizzy and exhausted from the spinning. Lars felt the look of trust his son gave him. He would, of course, never let go of his son, and Jens clearly knew it.

Lars slowed their spinning and finally brought his son to rest on his feet. He let go of Jens' hands and, out of exhaustion, they both fell backward into the flowers.

"It's so beautiful, isn't it, Father?" Jens said, lying flat on his back.

"I've never seen anything like this," Lars answered, enjoying the beauty of the flowers and the expanse of white.

It wasn't five minutes, though, before Lars was suddenly aware that he had no idea where they were or how they would get back to the path he was used to taking.

Lars (as well as the other villagers of Berglund) had always worked hard to keep out of difficult situations—the main philosophy behind their not taking risks. In his life so far, Lars had found it easy enough to walk "the path of least resistance" in both his work and personal relationships. The goal was to stay within the boundaries of his understanding and control, never to ask difficult questions of himself or others, and to stay away from situations where he might feel uncomfortable.

Since Inge's death, he'd had a feeling, at times—for example, when asking questions of people or when first climbing the mountain—that could be called uncomfortable. But he had never totally panicked until now. He'd come close to it just before seeing where Jens had landed when he'd jumped off the tree, but he hadn't had time to deal with his own panic.

Now, though, lost in this beautiful field of flowers, Lars found that he could not breathe and that his heart had momentarily stopped beating.

What should he do?

Then Lars touched the ring in his pocket and his panic subsided. He prayed for help, and came up with two options: Try to find the path they'd been on—the path he was most familiar with—or head straight toward the top of the mountain, hoping to cross the path to the secret meeting place in the process. Lars decided that, to save time, they would head toward the mountaintop. Somehow he was certain that they would find their way. He hoped, too, that Solveig would still be waiting.

Jens and Lars walked through the field of flowers until they reached an edge bordered with trees and brush. They turned around for one last look. From this view, the field looked even larger than before. They had obviously stumbled onto a plateau of some kind, on the side of mountain. The flowers appeared to drop off the field's far edge; it was impossible to see how far down the mountainside they continued.

"God is truly amazing," Lars said to his son.

"You mean God did all this?"

"Yes, Jens. He did," Lars answered. "The amazing thing is that I never saw this place any of the times I've been on the mountain. But *you* found it the very first time you came here."

"It is a gift, Father," Jens announced proudly.

"Yes, it certainly is," Lars replied. And he rubbed his hand over the top of his son's head.

Jens reached down and picked one of the beautiful flowers. "Can we bring some home to Mom?"

"Sure, we can."

The boy grabbed a handful of flowers, brushed the tiny black bugs from the stems, and carefully laid them in the backpack.

"Let's go find Solveig," Jens stated. Lars was amazed the boy actually remembered her name.

"God, thanks for sending gifts in all shapes and sizes," Lars thought to himself. And they turned and continued their journey up the mountain.

FIFTEEN ✑

"SOLVEIG, SOLVEIG. . ." Jens sang at the top of his lungs. *"We are on our way!"*

Lars jumped in, continuing Jens' melody. "We hope to find you sometime today."

They continued their trek farther and farther from the flower field and deeper into trees, rocks, and shrubs. The type of vegetation began to look familiar to Lars, but he still had no idea where they were in relation to the trail or Solveig's secret meeting place.

"Father?" Jens asked. "Do you think I really have to go to school today?"

Lars figured they were probably lost and there was no way of knowing when they'd make it back to the village. "In a way, Jens, with all you're learning, you're kind of going to school here on the mountain."

"Yeah! Like a field trip!"

"Very close to that, indeed," Lars remarked.

They continued their hike through the rough terrain, sometimes losing sight of the mountain's peak when tall pine trees or a ledge above blocked their view. When he *could* see the mountaintop, Lars adjusted their course.

"What's it going to be like when we get there?" Jens asked his father as they continued hiking.

"The place we're going," Lars began, "is a flat, open area

on the side of the mountain. People who climbed in the olden days would use it to rest, or even spend the night."

"Will there be pretty flowers there?"

"No, I haven't seen any flowers there before," Lars answered.

"That's too bad."

"Yes, it is, Jens."

"What do you do when you meet Solveig?" the boy asked.

"We talk," Lars explained. "She asks me questions and I try to answer them. Mostly, though, she gives me ideas about how to live life better."

"Will she tell *me* how to live better?"

"Probably not. That's my job." Lars surprised himself at the wisdom of these words. Where had it come from?

"I thought your job was a hammersmith, Father."

Lars laughed. "That's *one* of my jobs. But my most important job is you."

"Why am *I* a job?" Jens demanded, stopping in his tracks.

That comment made Lars stop as well. "Jens, I said it wrong. Sorry! You're not a job. You're not even a chore. It's just that it's my responsibility to raise you, and to not assume you're going to be all right no matter what I do. Does that make any sense?"

"Not really. But it's okay." Jens turned around and continued walking.

"How are those strong legs holding up?"

"Pretty good, Father."

Lars turned around to check the height of the sun in the sky. He figured they'd been on the mountain for about an hour and a half, an hour longer than it usually took him to get to the meeting place. He sang Jens' song again, "*Solveig, Solveig, we are on our way . . .*"

"Hey, Father, what's this?" Jens called out. Lars and his son had finally found what looked like a main trail through the part of the forest where they were. It ran across the path they were trying to take up the mountain and headed in two directions—to the left and the right.

"This is great!" Lars couldn't believe his eyes. The only problem they faced now was deciding which direction to go on the path.

Since Jens had run off their original trail to the right, Lars suggested they go to the left. He hoped it would cross his usual trail somewhere down the way.

"Good choice, Father," Jens said approvingly.

"Well, it *is* a choice," Lars thought to himself, not too certain about the quality of his decision.

They began their trek in this new direction. This trail cut across the face of the mountain instead of climbing upward. For a moment, Lars wondered if it might be connected to the path Solveig took each day.

"Father?" Jens asked.

"Yes, son?"

"I just want you to know," the boy continued, "that it's okay if I don't get to meet Solveig this morning."

"Why do you say that, Jens?"

"Because I'm having such a great time with you."

"That's awfully nice of you to say, Jens. I have to agree with you on that." Lars reached out to take Jens' hand. The path had just become wide enough for them to walk hand in hand beside each other, something they had not done often.

SIXTEEN ∽

LARS AND HIS SON continued along their newfound path for nearly thirty minutes, and then things began to appear even more familiar.

"I recognize these trees, Jens!" Lars said with excitement.

"Father, they look like every other tree we've seen," Jens answered.

"Yes, I know. But there's something different about these trees—maybe it's because they're getting smaller. The trees near the meeting place are small like these are."

They walked for a couple of minutes. Suddenly Lars started running.

"Jens, come on!"

"What is it, Father?" Jens ran to keep up with his father.

"We're here! The secret meeting place—we're here!"

Lars and Jens were standing right in the middle of Solveig's meeting place. Instead of joining up with the original trail, the path they'd found had brought them to the meeting place from below. Lars was relieved. Finding Solveig's meeting place meant they'd be able to return home safely and quickly, by heading down the trail Lars knew so well.

"This cannot be the secret meeting place, Father."

"Why is that?" Lars asked.

"There's no Solveig." Jens was good at pointing out the

obvious, although Lars had overlooked this fact because of his excitement over finding their goal.

"You're right," he agreed sadly.

Lars looked around the secret meeting place, thinking Solveig might have left a note or some kind of message for him. He didn't find anything, but he felt a Presence, not unlike the sense of encouragement and Love that he'd felt that first day when Solveig had touched him.

"Hey, Jens, why don't we sit down here for a minute?"

"Sounds great, Father," his son replied, with no apparent sign of exhaustion from their hike.

Lars took the backpack off and set it on the ground next to him. They sat with their backs against the side of the mountain and looked out over their village below.

"It sure is pretty," Jens said wistfully.

Lars was pleased that his son had an appreciation for the beauty of nature. He wondered how open the young boy would be to relationship. Touching the ring Solveig had given him, Lars said, "Son, you know how we go to church every Sunday?"

"Sure, Father. It's pretty boring, isn't it?"

"Well, yes, it is, now that you mention it."

They laughed together. Lars' face then turned serious as he tried to explain to his son what he'd recently learned. "That's why I'm so excited about finally being able to find out how to have an honest-to-goodness relationship with, uh . . . God."

Jens turned to his father and asked, " 'Honest to goodness'?"

"Yes, son," Lars continued. "Honest with myself, with you and Erik, with Mom, but most importantly, with God. Then God can change me with His perfect goodness."

"I think I'm getting hungry again, Father."

Lars chuckled, glad that Jens never let things get too deep or serious, or lost sight of the "more important" things in life, like food. He opened the backpack, nudged the flowers aside, and, ready now to eat something himself, he pulled out some of the food that remained from their first snack.

"Before we eat, Jens, how about we pray."

"Pray?" Jens wrinkled his forehead.

"Yes, pray. To God."

"Okay, Father. Whatever you say."

"Just tell God what you're thinking. It's pretty easy."

Jens didn't close his eyes or fold his hands in typical praying style—Lars was glad for that.

"God," Jens began, looking up to the sky. "This is really fun. I like my father." He looked at Lars and they smiled at each other. "I'm really happy not to be at school right now." He waited a minute, and then said to Lars, "That's all."

"Good job, son."

"Thanks, Father. Now you go."

Lars prayed in the same manner as his boy. "God, thank you for my wonderful son Jens, and Erik too, our beautiful daughter and sister, Inge, and their mother. You have given us so much. We cannot say thank-you enough. Thank you for keeping us safe this morning. Thank you for loving us." Lars looked at Jens and said, "That's all."

They both laughed

Looking out over the village, Jens munched his food and remarked, "Things look so small from up here!"

"It really is amazing," Lars said between bites of his sandwich, "how things seem so big when you're in the middle of them. But when you get a different view, things look so much smaller."

"Father, is that how it is for you when you go to work?"

"What do you mean, Jens?"

"When you leave us to go to work, do we get smaller because you're farther away?"

"Come here, son." Lars reached out and embraced his son. "You will never get smaller to me, no matter where I go or what I do."

Lars pulled Jens a little closer and finished with, "I keep you real big in my heart. Real big."

A nearby bird whistled its morning greeting. And somehow, Lars became aware that Solveig's departure after her usual prayer time at the secret meeting place, her not waiting for his arrival, had been for a reason. It had allowed Lars the chance to feel God's presence more directly, and it had given father and son this precious time together.

"How about we head back down to the village?" Lars asked his son after a while.

"Sounds good, Father."

Lars picked up the backpack and headed toward the path he usually took to return home.

"Good-bye, Solveig," Jens shouted.

"I don't think she can hear you, Jens," Lars laughed.

"Maybe not," Jens responded. "But just in case she can: *Good-bye, Solveig!*"

Lars smiled and added, "Thanks, Solveig." This special gift of her not showing up was a gift Lars would not soon forget.

SEVENTEEN

LARS AND JENS made it back to the village before too much of the morning had passed. Jens had to go home so that he could change his clothes and pick up his books before going to school. When they opened the front door, Lena ran from the kitchen to meet them.

"Oh, thank God you're still in one piece," she said as she grabbed Jens and hugged him tightly.

"Mother, it was so great," Jens said while freeing himself from her arms. "We saw so many things that were really pretty. I brought you some flowers!"

Lena's face lit up as he pulled the wilted daisies from the pack and handed them to her. "Thank you, Jens! That was so thoughtful! I'm sure a little water will freshen them right up. What else did you do up there?" She searched him with her eyes, trying to assure herself that he was truly not hurt by the expedition.

Jens grinned. "We hiked a lot," he said excitedly, trying to stand still to answer her. He succeeded for just about one minute. "And we got lost and we talked and we saw the village from up top and we prayed and . . ." By this time he had run off into his room, where Lars and Lena could no longer hear him.

"So?" Lena looked at Lars with curiosity.

"It was great," Lars assured her.

"But you got lost?"

"Not really." Lars rolled his eyes.

"Not *really*?" she pressed him, but she was smiling.

"Well, there *was* this one point," Lars whispered, "where I wanted to make it really exciting for Jens, and I pretended like we were lost."

"*Pretended?*" Lena clearly didn't believe the version her husband was offering her.

"Yes, it worked great!"

Jens ran back to his parents and announced, "I better get to school!" He started toward the door, but quickly turned to Lars and hugged him. "Thanks, Father."

"Thank you, Jens. I had a great time," Lars replied.

"See you later, Mother!" Jens added, and then, "Thanks!" when she handed him the vaguely worded note she'd written about Jens doing a task with his father, thus making the boy late for school.

Lars closed the door and noticed that Lena had a disappointed look on her face.

"What's wrong, Lena?" he asked.

"He didn't hug me." She sighed. "I wanted to hear all about the hike from him. But I guess he's more excited about telling everyone at school about what a great father he has— who took him up on the mountain."

"Most likely," Lars replied proudly.

Lena stood with her arms crossed, face glum.

Lars leaned into her, uncrossed her arms, placed them around his neck, and whispered, "How about a little coffee before I go to work?" He was hoping this might lead to an understanding of what was bothering her.

But Lena pulled her arms back down, turned, and started to walk away. "Not today. I have a lot to do."

Left standing alone near the front door, Lars tried to figure out what had just happened. Then he gave up. "Don't forget we're having dinner with Tomas and Lisbeth tonight," he finally called to her. And he closed the door behind him.

Lena, busy in the boys' bedroom, did not hear.

· · ·

Erik and the rest of the children in the village school were hard at work. They had already finished reading class, and were working on their arithmetic homework when Jens walked in.

Erik had obviously told someone that his brother had gone to the mountain because his classmates immediately began whispering to each other when they saw Jens arrive.

"How's your crazy father?" one student called out to him. This was followed by guffaws from the boys sitting near him.

"That's enough!" the teacher quickly responded. "Good morning, Jens," she continued. "Glad you could join us today."

Jens handed his teacher the required note, and went to his seat.

"We're delighted you came," a boy he passed whispered to Jens—a comment met with snickers from the boy's buddies.

"You should just be quiet," Jens said to the troublemakers.

"Ooh, I'm scared!" one boy said, followed by more laughter.

The teacher jumped in again. "Can someone tell me what's going on here?"

Jens and the other boys all sat quietly, refusing to answer.

"Fine," she said resignedly. "Then we will move on."

The class returned to their arithmetic lesson, but Jens knew this teasing would most likely be continued in the schoolyard. Somehow, he didn't care. He felt ready to deal with almost anything, now that he had romped in that meadow of daisies and been up to the secret meeting place.

Friday was generally the slowest day of the week for Lars. Even though he wasn't in his shop at the usual time, he didn't miss anything important. There was a note from Tomas attached to the shop door, with a reminder of their dinner plans for the evening. "Come hungry," the note stated.

"Not a problem!" Lars thought to himself.

While he worked on the projects of the day, he occasionally stopped to reflect on his morning with Jens on the mountain. He couldn't help but talk to God. "Thanks for the great time with my son. Thank you for continuing to point out to me how it's possible to see things differently. Please be with Lena today, and Erik, and especially Jens—I hope he'll begin to think differently about You because of today."

Lars sat in his shop and smiled—he was truly happy about how his life was changing. In fact, he was filled with joy. He knew God had been in complete control of his hike with Jens and had blessed them with a great time together.

If anyone had come into his shop that day and seen him this happy, they surely would have thought he was odd, maybe even up to something. But no one did come into the shop that day.

They missed the new, radiant Lars.

EIGHTEEN

NORMALLY, AT THE END of each school day, a group of children would gather in the yard for some kind of game. Jens always looked forward to this. When he and his brother came outside today, however, they stopped in their tracks. A group of boys were waiting for Jens—the same boys who had made fun of him in class. They were obviously not going to play a group game, and they were blocking the way Jens and Erik took to go home.

"Hello, Jens. How's the mountain man?" one boy called out. The other boys laughed or snickered.

Jens pretended he didn't hear them, and he took Erik's hand in his own and tried to keep walking.

"Where do you think you're going?" asked another.

"I'm going home to be with my family," Jens answered, looking down at his brother, whose face was filled with fear. "And I'm taking my brother with me."

"Your crazy mountain-climbing family?" someone yelled out, followed by more laughter.

Jens stopped, and dropped Erik's hand. He decided to tell these boys that mountain climbing had nothing to do with being crazy. That it had everything to do with being brave and courageous. He figured he had nothing to lose: They couldn't think he was any crazier than they already did.

"You don't have any idea what crazy is," Jens began.

"Yes, we do! *You* are!" one of the boys let out.

But then, unbelievably, most of the others actually stopped teasing and one boy asked what they all were wondering:

"What *is* crazy, then?"

"Crazy is being afraid of what you don't know," Jens continued.

"What are you talking about?" an older boy asked.

"You're not going to believe this. . . ." Jens mustered up all his courage and continued. "But this morning, when I went up the mountain with my father, we saw the most amazing things."

"You're making this up!"

"No, I'm not," he said simply.

"No, he's not," Erik added boldly.

"We saw the most beautiful field of wild daisies," Jens continued, "and we found a place where people from our village rested when they used to climb the mountain. We could look down on the village and see . . . how small everything is. It was incredible!"

The other boys clearly admired his enthusiasm about the climb, but they couldn't forget the unwritten rules of the village. Whoever tried to climb the mountain had to be looked down upon.

"So, you really climbed the mountain?" One of the boys said, and he stepped toward Jens.

"Yes, I did." Jens dropped his head, afraid to look this boy in the eye.

The boy stood there silent for a moment and then yelled right into Jens' face, "In that case, you *are* crazy!" Rallying the other boys, he cried out, "Let's get him!"

"Run, Erik! Run!" Jens yelled to his brother, who quickly obeyed his order.

Berglund's schoolyard had never seen a fight like this one. It was five against one. Jens did not stand a chance of escaping most of the punches and kicks. He figured his best defense was to lie on the ground and curl into a ball. He hoped his lack of resistance would keep things from becoming more intense, and that the boys would quickly grow bored. But the energy and clumsiness of the boys turned the fight into one big mass of arms and legs. No one could tell who was hitting whom. With each boy thinking *he* was fighting Jens, the fight grew worse.

From the bottom of the pile, Jens noticed that the boys were causing more damage to each other than they were to him. Soon he managed to squeeze out from under one of them and run away from the group.

He turned around for a brief second to watch the boys continuing their fight. He noticed his book bag lying on the ground near them and hoped it would still be there later. For now, he decided, it was best to run home as fast as he could.

"Eeewww!" Erik cried out when he saw his brother's face. Erik had run straight for Lars' shop and told him that Jens was "getting killed" on the schoolyard. The two of them met Jens at the end of the main road.

Jens had no idea how badly he'd been beaten until he saw the expressions on the faces of his brother and father. And on the faces of the silent people peering out the windows of their workplaces.

"Jens!" Lars grabbed his son and held him close. "What happened?"

Jens was crying now. Through his sobs he said, "Oh, Father. It was so *bad*."

Erik tried to explain everything to his father. "They said we're a crazy mountain-climbing family!"

"Is that true?" Lars asked Jens, inspecting the damage on his son's face.

"Yes," Jens answered softly.

Lars hugged his son, getting blood all over his work apron. "I'm so sorry, Jens. This is all my fault. I'm *so* sorry."

"No, it is not your fault, Father." Jens looked straight into his father's eyes. "They're all just afraid of what they don't understand."

Lars could only stop in wonder. Where had this son of his learned such wisdom beyond his years?

NINETEEN

FOR PARENTS, NOT MANY feelings are worse than the pain of seeing their own child hurting. And when the source of the hurt is something beyond the parents' control, anger can creep in and take over all other emotions.

Lars was very concerned about Jens and his well-being. But as he and his boys headed home, he could not stop thinking about the boys who had done this to his son. He was angry with them, but even more angry with their parents, who had obviously told the boys how to think about Lars and his family.

Walking hand in hand with Jens and Erik, Lars silently prayed, "God, I'm reminded how much I need Your help to make sure the things I'm teaching my boys are the things You want them to know." He continued, "Please remove the thoughts and feelings I have inside me that You don't want me to have. I cannot stand to think about angry words slipping out and staining my sons with hatred and spite."

Lars looked down at Jens' face, at the blood still running from a cut on his forehead. He pictured his son earlier that day running through the field of wild daisies. "He was so happy," Lars thought. "And now—"

Erik looked up at Lars and asked, "Father?"

"Yes, son?"

"Are you going to find out who did this to Jens and go beat up their fathers?"

Lars smiled. He actually pondered the thought for a moment before responding.

"I'm not sure what I'm going to do."

"You don't have to do a thing, Father," Jens replied.

"Yeah, Father," Erik added. "You don't have to do nothing."

Lars smiled and thought, "Sometimes the voice of God is most clearly heard through the voice of a child."

As they continued walking, Lars squeezed the hands of his boys a little tighter. Oddly enough, they were not in any hurry to get home. Some in the village may have viewed Lars' leisurely pace as careless. But they were together—the men of the family—walking a path they had never been on, straight down the middle of the main road.

Lars cherished the moment, knowing his boys felt completely safe by his side.

Lena was waiting for the boys to return from school when the front door opened and she heard Lars' voice call out, "Lena?"

She came out of the kitchen, wiping her hands on her apron, and saw Lars and the boys in the front hallway.

"Oh, my God in heaven!" she cried as she saw Jens' face covered with blood.

"He's okay," Lars quickly added.

"He's most certainly *not* okay," Lena answered, moving Jens into the kitchen where she could clean his wounds. "What happened?"

"Oh, Mother—" Jens began to explain.

Erik quickly jumped in. "Some boys at school don't know what they're afraid of. So they beat up Jens. I ran away *really fast.*"

Lena cleaned off Jens' face with a wet cloth, paying close attention to the cut above his right eyebrow and the one on his chin.

Jens continued, "There were just some boys at school . . ."

"Yes . . ." Lena said in a tone to urge him to say more.

"And they were making fun of me for climbing the mountain—telling me I was crazy."

She pulled him close and hugged him tightly. "You are *not* crazy!"

"I know, Mother. I know." Jens tried to wriggle out of his mother's tight grasp. She had unknowingly been putting pressure on his injuries.

"Are you hurt anywhere else?" Lena asked.

"Not really."

"Not really? What does that mean?"

"I'm fine," Jens said, and he walked out of the kitchen and toward his bedroom, with Erik close behind.

"For the first time in his life," Lars thought as he watched the scene from the doorway, "Jens obviously wants to keep some of his hurts to himself." He wondered how to explain to Lena that a boy sometimes needs to prove to himself that he doesn't need his mother to fix everything—

"He's just like his father," Lena said aloud, and she sighed.

"What do you mean?" Lars asked.

"Stubborn."

"Stubborn? What are you talking about?" Lars couldn't help reacting to her comment.

"He doesn't need any help."

"He doesn't need *your* help," Lars replied, forgetting to be gentle.

"Lars!" Lena was obviously offended.

"Sorry. But the boy is growing up, Lena," Lars began. "You and I are not always going to be there for him when he falls and scrapes his knee. He's learning to get up on his own. And as much as you might want to run and help him, Lena, you have to let him get up—*on his own*—just so he knows he can do it."

"But, Lars, the boy was just beaten up by a group of boys!"

"He did pretty well for himself, didn't he?" Lars said with a gleam in his eye.

Lena couldn't respond. She felt the truth of Lars' words about letting go, yet she also felt that her husband wasn't caring enough about their son.

"What are you going to do about this, Lars?" Lena asked matter-of-factly as she rinsed out the bloodstained washcloth.

"That I do not know," Lars replied. He actually did have an idea, but he wanted to wait and talk with Tomas about it that evening after their dinner together.

"Well, you'd better do something," Lena declared, and she wrung out the washcloth and hung it over the faucet to dry. "This wouldn't have happened if you hadn't climbed that crazy mountain and taken your son with you."

Lars stared at Lena. "What did you just say?"

"I said this wouldn't have happened if you hadn't climbed that crazy mountain—"

"Oh, really." Lars couldn't believe what he was hearing. "So, is that how you really feel?"

"Yes, it is," Lena responded, looking straight at Lars. "I can't help wondering what it is you're trying to prove. And who you are trying to prove it to."

"I'm not trying to prove anything, Lena!" Lars replied strongly. "The only thing I want to prove is that life doesn't have to be the way it is in Berglund—that life can be much, much more! These patterns of doing everything the same way, year after year, has only worn ruts deep into the soil of this village. I'm not going to settle for that any longer."

Lars took a deep breath and continued. "If rising above the crowd means simply climbing out of the rut, that is what I am going to do! No matter what other people think!" Lars sat down at the table, exhausted yet proud of the words he had spoken, and surprised at his boldness.

He looked at Lena to see what her response would be.

She was silent.

Lars leaned toward her and asked, "Will you please come with me?"

"Where are you going *now*?"

"I'm climbing out of the rut—and I want you to come with me. Will you come?"

"I can't answer that right now, Lars," Lena replied. "I need more time!" She threw up her hands and walked out of the kitchen.

"Please?" Lars called out to her.

There was no answer.

He felt in his pocket and touched his ring. He prayed, "God, if You are here with me, I certainly don't feel it. Is that how You want it to be?"

He didn't hear or feel any response.

"I guess it is," Lars concluded.

He placed his head down on the table and began to cry.

TWENTY

SOON IT WAS TIME for the Hansen family to get ready for their dinner with Tomas and Lisbeth. Lars had reminded the boys to get ready and had begun to change his own clothes when Lena stepped into the bedroom and asked, "When were you going to tell me about our dinner tonight?"

"I thought I told you about it Wednesday night after Tomas asked me," Lars answered. "And I reminded you this morning—"

"Thank goodness I ran into Lisbeth at the market today. She filled me in on your plans."

"Lena, I'm so sorry," Lars said to his wife. "This was supposed to be fun."

"I'm sorry, too, Lars," Lena responded sadly.

Gently, Lars said, "Can we go and just have a good time tonight?"

"I guess we'll have to," she said, and she sighed.

Lars stopped and watched his wife brush her hair. He shook his head, feeling helpless. Then he headed for the boys' room and called out, "Boys? Are you just about ready?"

"Yes, Father!" Erik answered.

"Jens?" Lars asked when he reached the doorway to their room.

"Yes, sir?" Jens softly replied.

"Are you okay?" Lars leaned on the door frame and watched his son.

"Yes, Father. I'm okay." He was tying his shoelace conscientiously.

"Jens," Lars said quietly, and his son looked up at him and waited for what his father had to say. "I'm very proud of you."

"Thanks, Father. I'm proud of you, too."

"Me too, Jens," Erik said boldly to his older brother. "I'm proud of you, too."

Jens looked over Erik and laughed. "Thanks, Erik. Thanks a lot."

Lena came and joined them in the hall. "Ready?" she asked with a resolute smile.

"Let's go, then," Lars stated. "We'll pick up Jens' book bag on the way."

Dinner with Tomas and Lisbeth was the usual potatoes and meatballs. No one complained, since it was a favorite meal of the entire Hansen family.

Lisbeth and Lena did not say much at the table, but after everyone had finished eating, they collected the dirty dishes and carried them into the kitchen together. Jens and Erik had found their favorite card game and were content playing in the living room.

"Tell me again why Lars is climbing the mountain," Lisbeth asked Lena as they began washing the dishes. She had been told something about the trip when she'd commented on the cut on Jens' forehead.

"I don't know, exactly," Lena began. "He says it's about wanting to be a better husband and father. But if what he does gets our boy in trouble at school, I think it's time to figure out a better way."

"I agree," Lisbeth said as she handed a plate to Lena. "But I have to say, I do admire his bravery. God knows, you've been waiting for years for him to pay more attention to the family!"

"Yes, but I never thought it would turn out quite like this."

The women returned to the dining area as Tomas and Lars were getting up from the table.

"Going somewhere?" asked Lena, more relaxed than she'd been in a while.

"Yes, dear," Lars responded. "Tomas and I are going to take a little walk."

"Okay, *dear*," Lena returned with a grin.

Tomas moved to Lisbeth and kissed her, saying, "Thank you so much for dinner. It was wonderful. We'll be back soon."

The men went outside, while the women continued to clean up after the evening's meal.

Lars and Tomas sat on a bench in the front yard and stared up at the star-filled sky.

Tomas spoke the first words. "It sure is beautiful."

"Yes, it sure is," Lars answered slowly.

Tomas could clearly see that Lars had something very heavy on his mind. He let several moments of silence pass between them.

"Your boys are sure getting big!" After he said this, he turned toward Lars and saw a tear fall down his cheek.

"Why is it, Tomas, that boys are allowed to grow up physically," Lars questioned, "but they get in trouble if they let their minds go too far outside of the borders of this village? It's almost as if this little place we live in is a jail."

Tomas did not know how to respond.

"With our ways of doing things . . . we think we're protecting ourselves," Lars continued. "But we're actually caging ourselves in!"

"If you could do anything you wanted to do, what would it be?" Tomas asked his friend.

"What do you mean?" Lars turned and looked at Tomas.

"I mean, if you could have this perfect world that you're talking about, what would it actually look like?" Tomas looked at Lars for an answer.

"Tomas, I'm not talking about having a perfect world,"

Lars replied, sounding more frustrated than ever. "I'm not a politician!"

"Calm down, Lars. I'm on your side," Tomas said. "I'm not trying to argue with you. I just want to understand more about what you're thinking."

"I'm sorry."

"So, what are you thinking?" Tomas kept pressing.

"I'm thinking about God—for the first time in my life," Lars said softly.

"This is about *God*?" Tomas sounded surprised.

"Yes, it is. It's *all* about God, Tomas." Lars explained. "I've found that God wants to relate to me personally, and also with you, with everyone. As I'm learning more and more about what that actually means, I'm finding that my life is changing. My selfish way of thinking about everything is being replaced by thoughts of love and compassion for my family and everyone around me." Lars finished and looked straight into his friend's eyes.

Tomas was stunned.

"That's all I want to do now," Lars continued. "I want to keep seeking after what God has, and allow Him to change me into what He wants me to be."

"Aren't you happy with who you are now?" Tomas asked.

"I thought I was! I really did! And then Inge died. And then God started showing me how I was so self-centered and how I was actually hurting the people around me. . . ." Lars leaned back on the bench.

Tomas was still curious. "So God is in the business of showing us everything that's wrong with us?"

Lars stopped and thought for a minute how to respond. Touching his ring, he said, "God is in the business of showing us who He is. As we see who God is, we're able to see how *we* really are. It is like this: He cleans the dirt off the window of our soul, revealing more truth about us. If I want anything good to come of my life, I'm going to need His help."

Tomas let out a huge sigh and looked up at the stars. "Lars, I don't completely understand what you're talking about, but

I would like to. So that I can be the kind of friend I would like to be to you."

Lars smiled at his friend. "Thank you, Tomas. You are, without question, *nice.*"

They laughed together, unaware of the shooting star that just passed overhead.

TWENTY-ONE

TOMAS AND LARS HAD BEEN friends ever since they were little children growing up together in Berglund. Even though they didn't always agree on everything, they maintained their closeness through a shared sense of humor. Tomas' patience and compassion probably had a lot to do with why their relationship continued. It also helped that their wives were good friends who spoke frequently about husbands. Lisbeth listened to Lena's talk about her children, and responded helpfully, even though she and Tomas had never had any children of their own.

The men were continuing their conversation under the stars when Tomas asked, "Do you think you need to do something about the boys in the schoolyard?"

"I really want to," Lars answered, "but I'm not sure what I should do. As it is, I'm not exactly the most liked person in town."

"There's no contest going on."

"What do you mean, Tomas?"

"There's no contest to see who can be the most liked."

"Are you saying I've dug my hole deep enough as it is, and that I probably cannot go any deeper?"

"No, Lars. I'm saying it's probably more important for you to stand up for what you believe than it is for you to be liked."

Lars was surprised that Tomas would encourage him to take such a risk.

"Where did that come from, Tomas?" Lars wondered aloud.

"I can tell that you're very passionate about what you believe. If you really think what you have to say will be helpful to the rest of the village, I highly recommend that you say it."

"You mean that, Tomas?"

"Yes, I do. But don't do something just to make yourself feel better. Or to prove to others that you know things no one else does."

Lars thought about Tomas' words. His anger and frustration over his son's situation turned into nervous anticipation.

"I'm a little scared," Lars admitted.

"Good."

"Good?"

"Yes, it's good for you to be scared," Tomas replied.

"You really think so?"

"No question."

Lars asked him, "What are you doing Sunday?"

"During the day?"

"In the morning," Lars said.

"Well, of course, we will be at church, and then—"

Lars interrupted, "Good."

"Good?" Tomas asked.

"Yes, I'm going to need your help."

"Okay, Lars. But no fighting!"

Lars quickly answered, "I'll come up with something else, then."

The two friends laughed together under the stars.

TWENTY-TWO ∾

SOLVEIG HAD NEVER SAID anything to Lars about not meeting on the weekends. He hoped she would be there at sunrise, even though today was Saturday. He was anxious to talk to her about what had happened the day before. His body was now in the habit of waking up automatically just before the sun rose.

Lars and Lena had not spoken about anything important when they returned home from dinner the previous evening. Still, he bent over and kissed her on the cheek as he was leaving this morning.

"I love you, Lena. And I'm sorry," he whispered into her ear. She did not stir—he wasn't sure if she was asleep, or just ignoring him.

Lars was relieved when he arrived at Solveig's secret meeting place and saw the old woman down on her knees, in the same position she'd been in when he'd first met her. The sight of her made Lars feel completely comforted, as if he had just run home to his mother after a hard day at school.

Even though he had been extremely close with his father, there was something special about his mother's ability to calm and soothe him. It might have been her loving eyes, or the way she listened to anything he had to say, or her homemade pies or cookies. But most of the time, it was also her just being there that helped him solve most of his problems.

That was how he felt now, seeing Solveig after the emotional ups and downs of the previous day. It reminded him so much of his mother, he could almost smell a fresh apple pie baking in the oven.

Solveig looked up and saw Lars. Her eyes looked with favor on him, as she slowly beckoned to him.

Walking toward her, Lars cried out with joy, "Solveig!"

"Hello . . . my dear boy," she replied slowly, as though sounding out each word with great care.

Lars was suddenly frightened. Not only did it seem hard for Solveig to talk, she was moving quite slowly, as if each turn of her head or arm caused her pain.

"Solveig, are you all right?" Lars asked with concern, moving even closer to her side. She put her finger up to her mouth to silence him.

"Today . . . we use few words." Solveig could still smile her radiant, toothy grin, but Lars saw deep pain in her eyes.

He kept talking. "But there's so much I need to tell you, and so much I need you to tell me." His mind began racing. He was deeply concerned about Solveig and what was happening to her. At the same time, he desperately wanted to get her advice on the things going on his life.

She again put her finger up to her mouth.

"Listen," she said to him.

"But I don't hear anything!" Lars answered impatiently.

Solveig reached for Lars' hand and placed it over his heart. He could feel it beating very quickly.

"You want me to listen to my heart? Is that what you want, Solveig? But I *have* been listening to my heart, and it has only got me into a lot of trouble."

She tried calming him, but her difficulty in speaking was only making Lars more confused and impatient. "Lars, life is very short," she continued. "You know I love you very much."

"Yes, Solveig. I know that. I love you, too."

She continued, "But my love for you is very small compared to how much God loves you. That is the secret of all secrets."

Lars liked the thought of God loving him, but he didn't understand how that was supposed to affect his life. "Solveig, what does God's love matter, when bad things happen to me and to my son?" he questioned.

"It matters—" She paused to catch her breath, and then finished her thought. "—everything."

"But, Solveig—"

She again quieted him with her finger to her lips.

"Even when you don't feel it, or it doesn't seem to be enough for what you're going through . . ." Solveig's voice became more and more quiet. Her eyes slowly closed, and her head dropped to her chest. Lars wanted to reach for her head and hold it upright. He wanted to believe she was only falling asleep, but he knew there was something more serious happening.

"Solveig!" He placed his hand on her arm.

She opened her eyes and looked at Lars with as much strength as she could gather before she spoke. "Love . . . Him . . . back. . . ."

Solveig's body then slumped over into the position she'd been in when Lars had met her, looking as if she was praying.

"Please, go now," she whispered from her crouched position.

Lars would not let go. "I cannot go now, Solveig. What is wrong? How can I help you?"

"Please go."

"But, Solveig!" Lars pleaded.

"I will see you again"—She took a deep breath and continued—"soon."

Lars did not want to leave the secret meeting place with Solveig in that condition. He did not understand why she didn't want him there any longer. But he knew there was no point in making things harder on her.

The tears stung his eyes as he forced himself to leave Solveig behind. He stood up, turned, and began walking away when he heard her whisper again, "Love . . . Him . . . back."

He had no idea how to actually begin loving God. But her words rang true in his heart. Lars knew he would be willing to spend the rest of his life trying to figure it out, even if he never saw Solveig again.

TWENTY-THREE ❧

THE HIKE DOWN THE MOUNTAIN that day was the most difficult it had ever been for Lars. Not for any physical reason, but because of all the thoughts spinning inside his head. He had hoped to receive some direction from Solveig about how to handle the resentment he felt from the villagers, as well as from his wife. He felt completely helpless with both of these situations.

"God, is this what You want?" he prayed out loud to God. "You want me to feel helpless and not able to do anything about my situation?"

What happened next stopped Lars in his tracks. For the first time since he'd started talking with God, he heard an answer! It was not an actual voice like the one he had hoped for; rather, it was as if the answer had been whispered in his ear. More specifically, though, he felt the words in his heart.

"On your own, you *are* helpless," the heart-voice said. "Now that you realize this, I can finally use you."

"Use *me*?" Lars answered.

"The things you want to do in your life, I also want to do. But in a deeper, more significant way than you can even imagine."

"How will You do that?"

"Trust Me," he heard the voice say.

"But what am I supposed to do?" Lars wondered.

"Trust Me."

Lars did not think trusting seemed like a very practical way to accomplish anything. "Yes, God, but couldn't I do so much more than that?" he began. "I could build houses, or construct statues for You. I could even travel thousands of miles past the mountain, to go places You want me to go. Just tell me what You want me to do."

A third time he heard, "Trust Me."

Lars fell to his knees, his body and mind overtaken by humility.

"God, please forgive me," he cried out, "for thinking I have anything to give You. All I have is from You. Anything I want to accomplish in my life can be done only by You. If showing You that I love You means trusting You, this is what I will do."

With this promise, Lars began the journey of his life—one that would eventually lead him through this world and into eternity.

TWENTY-FOUR

SUNDAY CAME TO BERGLUND, and the villagers found their way into the church sanctuary for the morning service. Lars and his family sat in their usual seats in the fourth row from the front, left side. Gunnar Veigelsen, who had been playing the same few songs over and over for most of his eighty years, played the organ. The congregation sat down after the opening hymn and one of the elders began reading the Scripture passage of the day.

Lars was having difficulty listening to what was being read. He was busy looking around at the different families with young boys, wondering which ones had beat up Jens. Each time he spotted a boy who looked about Jens' age and who had bruises or cuts on his face, he looked also at the boy's father. It was usually a man whom Lars had never spent any time with, Lars realized, or someone who didn't appear to be the least bit concerned about anything Lars did. He wished Jens had told him who the boys were, but Jens had chosen not to tell.

Lena cleared her throat to get Lars' attention. He looked at her and she signaled for him to turn around and focus on what was being said from the pulpit. It was just as if he were twelve years old again, with his own mother scolding him in church.

Pastor Sundqvist began this week's sermon on Hell by

talking about how there are some people in this world who are not the least bit afraid of spending eternity in the pit of fire.

"How can this be?" the pastor asked. "It is simple, my dear ones. People get used to the smell of smoke. They get used to the heat of the fire."

Lars squirmed in his seat, knowing that if he was going to address the entire village at one time, this would be the perfect place.

"Too many people have been playing with fire during their lives here on Earth," Pastor Sundqvist continued. "They have lost all feeling in their hands and in their hearts."

"Amen!" someone in the back of the church seemed to shout. Or was it someone outside the church?

Lars turned his head to the right and looked at Lena. She was intently listening to the sermon. He looked down at his boys sitting next to him. Jens looked up at him.

Lars whispered to him, "Pray for me."

Jens was not sure what his father meant, but saw him immediately slip out of the pew and into the left aisle of the church. Lars walked straight to the pulpit.

Nobody ever moved during the pastor's sermon, much less went up to the pulpit. People all over the congregation began whispering to each other.

The pastor continued, "And these people have friends who are just throwing wood on the fire—" He stopped midsentence when he saw Lars approaching him.

Lars whispered into Pastor Sundqvist's ear, "I am sorry, pastor. I will just be a minute."

The pastor whispered back, but not so quietly, as if to prove that he could maintain control over any situation, "Do you think this could wait until I am finished here?"

Lars ignored the pastor's question and turned to face the congregation. Almost everyone stared at him in disbelief and amazement. He noticed that several mouths had dropped completely open.

He took a deep breath. "Good morning, everyone," he said solemnly. "Excuse me for interrupting. But I am very concerned about what is happening among us here in the village. All of you know by now that I have been climbing the mountain. Yes, I realize the risk I am taking. But I am taking that risk, not because I am crazy, but because I desire my life to be something more than what it has become.

"We have been doing the same things over and over for too long. The ruts we have dug for ourselves have hindered our vision from seeing anything outside our own little village. We rarely even talk to each other! But we do talk within our homes, and your children have picked up some of the things you have been saying to each other.

"That is how I found out about your feelings, by seeing what some of your children did to my son after school on Friday."

The church was deathly silent. Pastor Sundqvist took his seat behind the pulpit. Lars looked around and stared directly into the eyes of anyone who was watching. It appeared most people were watching, and waiting for what else he had to say.

"In the process of trying to discover what life outside the village has to offer, I have found that God wants to have a personal relationship with me—and with all of you."

More people began to murmur. The pastor shifted uncomfortably in his seat.

"We come to this church every week," Lars continued. "But what does it matter in our lives? Not a whole lot. I am not standing up here today to try and get all of you to be open-minded to our differences, although that would be a good start for some of us. This is about setting our minds on things Above—getting to know God, letting Him get through to us, and allowing Him to open our minds and hearts and fill them with His Spirit. With His wisdom, love, and hope. Then, when we let Him keep us filled, all of our lives will be deeply changed for the better."

Someone shouted out from the back, "What if we don't want to change?"

Lars smiled. "That's a good question."

He cleared his throat and looked at Lena, who was watching with wide eyes. Inge's face appeared in Lars' mind. He thought for a moment about how much his daughter's death had been affecting him and Lena, perhaps without their fully realizing it.

"Change is difficult," he continued. "It stirs things up—things that have been comfortable up to now. I don't blame you if you don't want to change. But if you hear nothing else from me today, please hear this. There is more to this life than many of us are now experiencing.

"I'm not saying that bad things will stop happening to us if we change. But what I have found is that bad things don't matter in the same way. I now have a peace that goes even beyond my circumstances, a joy that transcends my earthly understanding, because of a Love who accepts me unconditionally. I'm only just beginning to understand what all this means. But I'm on my way, and I would like to take anyone with me who would like to go."

He looked around the room, and saw people whispering to each other and shaking their heads.

"Are there any people here who can feel in their hearts what I'm talking about? Is there anyone here who maybe doesn't completely understand what I'm talking about but wants to find out more? If so, you are the person I'm looking for. Anyone?"

Lars let a moment of silence pass. Suddenly Jens jumped up on the pew and shouted, "I'll go with you, Father!"

Erik then jumped up on the pew as well. "Me too, Father!" he added.

As nervous as Lena felt, she looked at her boys, and then at her husband. She was amazed at his passion and conviction. Though she still had many doubts and questions, she knew her love for her husband was stronger than any pride. She stood and said, "I will go with you, Lars."

A woman gasped from across the room.

Karl Henie stood up as though he would come, but then he looked around and sat down again.

Mayor Tomas and his wife, Lisbeth, immediately stood up, holding hands. "We will go with you, too."

Tears came to Lars' eyes at this sight. The most important people in his life were standing up with him. Another minute passed and no one else stood.

"Is that it?" Lars asked.

Sven Jorgensen, the locksmith who had his shop across from Lars, stood up and said sternly, "You can go your own way, Lars Hansen, but the rest of us are going to stick together!"

Lars answered, "I'm not going 'my own' way. I've been doing that my whole life. I'm deciding now to go *another* way, one that has nothing to do with me but everything to do with God."

Jorgensen sat back down. Lars stood still for another minute, then he started walking down the middle aisle toward the back door. Lena and the boys and Tomas and Lisbeth followed him down the aisle.

"Have a nice time on the mountain!" someone jeered from the crowd.

Lars stopped when he heard those words. "Please know this: The mountain is always there for you," he began. "If you ever change your mind, the opportunity for you to climb it will be there. And I would be glad to walk beside you every step of the way."

Lars, Lena, Jens, Erik, Tomas, and Lisbeth walked out the door, down the steps, and into the bright sunlight of the morning.

TWENTY-FIVE

ON THE WAY OUT of church, Lars heard the same heart-voice he'd heard on the way down the mountain. The words were very clear, but the reason for them was difficult for Lars to understand. The voice said, "Get ready to leave."

Lars' response was, "Leave what?"

To which he heard nothing.

The more he thought about it, the more he understood how very disturbing to many people his words had been. He had no idea how they would respond to him or to his family after they had more time to think about what he'd said.

Lars invited Tomas and Lisbeth over for dinner after church, but they respectfully declined, figuring Lars and Lena could use some time alone to think about the morning's events. They made plans to talk the next day about when to go up the mountain together.

The Hansens did not say much to each other on the way home, or after they arrived there. When they all sat down to eat, little Erik broke the silence by saying, "Church was fun today!"

"It sure was," Lars answered, rubbing his hand over Erik's head.

Lars decided to take a risk at the dinner table. He asked his family if they could please prepare to leave their home.

Lena immediately responded with, "What are you talking about?"

He took a deep breath and answered her. "I don't know exactly what I mean, but I upset a lot of people this morning. I have a strong sense that we should be ready for anything."

"It's a real-life adventure!" Jens said enthusiastically.

Lars got more specific after they'd finished eating. "I want each of us to pack one bag of whatever we'd want with us if we had to suddenly leave here. Please, let's just do it, okay? So that, if we *do* have leave quickly, we'll be ready. If I'm wrong, I'm wrong. But if I'm right, we'll be glad we did it."

It was a difficult task for everyone. It forced them to look at the long-term value and importance of everything they owned. Surprisingly, very little was packed. Certainly much less than they would have tried to pack before Inge's death. They did not know if or when they were going to leave, or why, but they were prepared.

That evening, with their four bags packed and sitting in their until-then-unused addition, Lars gathered the family in the living room.

"I want to say thank-you to each of you for trusting me enough to do this," Lars began, his face glowing in the light of the several candles he had lit. "I know this has been a confusing time for all of us. But I have incredible hope that, starting today, life is going to be better than we could ever imagine."

"Are we going to see God?" Erik innocently asked.

Jens punched him on the shoulder, thinking his question was dumb.

Lars answered, "Yes, I hope so. Someday. I don't know what it's going to be like when we see Him, but I believe we *will* see Him."

He reached out his hand to Lena on his left and Jens on the right. Jens took Erik by the hand, as did Lena.

"But until we see Him, Erik, let's keep talking to Him."

For the first time, they each took turns praying aloud as a family. When they finished, they all sat quietly together, still holding hands in the glow of the candlelight. Then, to keep that feeling of togetherness, they put out the candles and "camped out" in Lars' addition, where they told family stories and sang favorite songs until they fell asleep.

In the middle of the night, a loud bang in the front of the house awakened Lars and Lena and the boys. He rushed out to find the living room and kitchen completely engulfed in flames. The first thing he did was thank God—for stirring his heart to prepare his family for a quick exit, and for prompting them to sleep that night in the addition.

"Jens, Erik!" Lars called out. "Lena! Grab your things!"

The family had no trouble getting out of the burning house safely. They simply dropped their bags out one of the addition's windows, then Lars helped Lena climb out, and he handed the boys down to her before he followed.

Out on the lawn, Lars put his arms around his family. They stood together in the glow of the flames, silently watching the front walls and roof burn. A small crowd of sleepy villagers stood at a distance, also watching. They were fearful that burning ashes or sparks might fly onto their own houses, but even more afraid to help quench the fire.

After a few minutes Lars embraced his family and murmured in a tone of wonder, "It's really true!"

"What's true, Lars?" Lena asked, moving closer into her husband's arms while she held on to their children.

"It's only a house! It doesn't matter if it burns. It's the love we have for each other—like the love I have from you, and you, and you"—he squeezed Lena and Jens and Erik as he said this—"that matters."

Lena smiled in agreement, the flames lighting up her face.

Lars continued in an awed tone, as though thinking aloud, unable to stop sharing the immensity of what he was finally understanding. "The love we have for each other cannot be lost. It's in our hearts, where no one can touch it! Inge's love for us is there too." Lars wanted so badly to explain what was suddenly becoming so clear to him. "Thank you, God, for keeping us safe. And for showing me, finally, that I'm the only one who can hurt the love You have in mind for me. . . . Help us all to understand that this love You want for us is so much deeper than the best love we've ever felt for one another." Lars felt filled, now, with the power of all the love he had been too stubborn to notice. Perhaps it was only the warmth from the house fire, but perhaps it was more than that. He felt a warm glow begin to move from his heart, through his body, and then down through his arms and into those he embraced.

Lena felt something new, too. For the first time since Inge's death, she felt truly loved. The ups and downs of family life no longer mattered to her.

Jens and Erik smiled. They each felt the strength of their family's love that, at least for the moment, was winning out over the ignorant hatred that had caused their house to be torched.

An unexpected peace filled the Hansen family. They embraced and fell to their knees in prayer.

"Your house is on fire and all you can do is pray?" taunted one of the unmoving villagers. "That's the dumbest thing I've ever seen!"

Suddenly Karl Henie approached the Hansen house. With him were many men, women, and children, all carrying tools and supplies to help fight the fire. They immediately went to work, using buckets of water and dirt to help put out the flames. Lars and his family, immobilized by the fullness of what they were feeling, stood back and gratefully watched their neighbors.

"We can still save the house!" one cried out.

Karl ran over to Lars and whispered in his ear, "Thank you for what you said in church this morning. But please don't tell anybody I told you that!" Then he quickly ran off to continue fighting the fire.

A short time later, another man approached Lars. "I don't know how you did it, but thanks for finally saying what I've been thinking all along. You are a brave man."

Before they were finished, nearly a dozen men and women

had come over to Lars to express their appreciation for what he had done at church.

The house was not completely destroyed. Still, it would require quite a lot of rebuilding.

Tomas appeared through the crowd that had gathered, and invited the Hansens to come to his house. Lisbeth met them at the door with warm cocoa and blankets to help take away the early morning chill.

Lars noticed the sun begin to rise, and he felt compelled to go meet Solveig.

"I shall return soon," he promised Lena. And she replied with a quick hug.

He began to run down the road toward the mountain. He was running with greater confidence and strength than he had ever felt. He knew for sure that Solveig would be proud of how he had handled this situation. He anticipated her "Well done!" so much that he could already picture her warm eyes drawing him into an embrace.

But when he arrived at their meeting place, Solveig was nowhere to be found.

"*Solveig! Where are you?*" His words echoed off the mountain wall behind him. He tried again. "*Solveig!*"

As the echo died out, he heard sweet, joyful music floating through the air. It was the sound of Solveig's singing!

He ran down the path she usually came from, only to find that the path ended a short way past the meeting place. There was nowhere for him to go, yet he could still hear her beautiful singing.

Lars ran back to the meeting place and sat down. Suddenly all went quiet. No music, only the wind gently blowing through the nearby bushes.

He no longer felt the confidence and enthusiasm he'd had on the climb up the mountain just a short time before. He felt a heavy weight upon his shoulders instead, so he touched his ring and asked for help, hoping for direction.

Slowly, he realized that he would never see Solveig again. A tear came to his eye and he sat facing Berglund while a massive ache filled his heart.

The sun inched its way over the horizon, and revealed a clear view of his burned-out house. The streets were quiet, for all the villagers had settled back into the safety of their own homes.

When the sun got to a certain level, a ray of its light hit something hidden in a cleft of the rock behind him. It glinted off whatever it had found and refracted onto the bushes in front of Lars. He turned and found a small silver box placed in a niche in the mountain's face.

Lars quickly removed the string around the box and lifted off the lid. Inside were a letter and a bag of seeds. Falling to his knees he read:

> *Lars,*
>
> *Well done, my son. I am very proud of you. I wish I could be there with you right now to celebrate. It has become very clear to me that our Heavenly Father desires me to be with Him.*
>
> *My first thought was one of regret at never being able to see you again on the mountain. But that thought is quickly erased by the thought of seeing my Lord face to face.*
>
> *We do only see through a glass dimly while here on Earth. But these last few days have been a time of cleansing, polishing, and refining for me. The glass has become so clear that I can see our Lord as if He is right in front of me, arms reaching out, calling my name. His face is filled with a love that I cannot find words to describe to you.*
>
> *The truths I shared with you here in this mountain's secret meeting place are now yours to take with you, wherever you go. Don't keep them a secret. God has been here with us, but He has also been with you all along. Even before we met, He was with you, patiently longing for you to acknowledge Him. Your life can now be an act of worship, meeting with Him here or wherever you are, resting in His love and grace.*
>
> *I leave you this bag of seeds as a gift of hope. You've learned a*

lot over the past few weeks, and the thing I am most proud of is how hope has come alive in your heart. Use these seeds to prove to others that God can take some dirt and a few small seeds and create something incredibly beautiful.

I long to tell our Father how proud I am of you.

— Sol

With tears of joy now, mingled with his sadness, Lars folded the letter and placed it against his chest. He planted half the seeds there, in the secret meeting place, and took the rest with him.

On his way down the mountain, Lars started dreaming about how Berglund could become new for each of the villagers, perhaps a place where choices were limitless, where villagers could think beyond their small surroundings, and where they would be encouraged to find their own secret meeting places.

In this new Berglund his children would be able to start to dream about what they wanted to be, for they would not have to be hammersmiths unless they chose to be. His wife could find new meaning in the village, if she chose, perhaps by helping other people. Lars did not care so much about what he would do. He knew who he was going to *be*, and that was all that mattered in this new life he hoped for. The Hansens would rebuild their house into a new home with just the right number of rooms. He would create a new garden where he could plant Solveig's seeds. But most of all, the new Berglund would be a place where everyone would be free to be graciously good to each other.

Lena was waiting for Lars at the bottom of the mountain. Her faced beamed with pride and love at the sight of him.

"Tomas and Lisbeth are watching the boys. How about finally taking me up to the meeting place, you crazy mountain climber?" she asked.

Lars grabbed her and held her tight. "One time together, my love. Tomorrow we'll take the boys and Tomas and Lisbeth. We won't need to climb the mountain after that. Our secret meeting place can be wherever we make it." He looked into her eyes and continued, "Here, sweet one. Before we climb the mountain and I tell you about all that Solveig gave me, come with me."

They walked down the village path to the church, past the pastor's home, and into the town cemetery. Lena could see that they were heading to little Inge's earthly resting place, but something looked different to her.

"Lars, where did that daisy come from?" she asked as they reached the headstone and knelt down together.

"I can only imagine," he replied with a grin. And he took four seeds out of the bag from Solveig and planted them deep in the soil next to the flower already blooming there.

AFTERWORD

AT THE END of *The Secret Meeting Place,* Lars is really only at the beginning of his journey. He has desire, but he hasn't yet learned to be there fully for others. Desire is, indeed, an excellent first step. For once desire is acted on, the goal will be achieved.

Like the villagers of Berglund, we all choose, at times, to look at only the familiar, self-serving aspects of life. We rarely take our eyes off ourselves, our families, our immediate neighbors, and what we think we need to accomplish today.

This is why, like Lars, we so often feel as though something crucial is missing from our lives.

The secret is out: We all need a secret meeting place—a special place and time where the Spirit of God can remind us how to put priorities in their proper light.

Why not follow Lars' example, and find your own secret meeting place? That is indeed what Lars would wish for you.

It is the authors' hope that you will visit a quiet place each day. And there that you will learn to draw inspiration from God, not from any particular earthly teacher. And then, that you will reflect on those inspirations and try to put them into action.

If you make this daily meeting a most important priority of your day, the spiritual food you find there will nourish your faith, courage, and ability to love more truly.

And your life, which could have been only ordinary, will become truly extraordinary.

ABOUT THE AUTHORS

CECIL O. KEMP JR. is a Christian and devoted husband, father, and grandfather living in Franklin, Tennessee. Formerly a CPA and corporate executive in a publicly held company, in 1982 he and his wife, Patty, cofounded a successful financial planning and investment advisory company. They sold it in 1998, and since then Cecil has written eight personal growth and inspirational books, including the Pinnacle Award–winning *Wisdom Honor & Hope*, and the highly acclaimed *7 Laws of Highest Prosperity*. He is also the creator and principal writer of The Hope Collection, a heartfelt series of sixteen full-color devotional-like gift books.

Cecil is a financial and business expert and consultant, the pioneer of Emotional Intelligence Coaching, and a keynote speaker. Call his agent, toll free 1-800-728-1145, if you have an interest in working with him in one or more of these roles or in buying his books in large quantities at substantial discounts for use as gifts, customer rewards, marketing and sales premiums, and/or educational tools.

MARK SMEBY is a Christian living in Franklin, Tennessee. An accomplished author, actor, songwriter, and singer, Mark's creative efforts have received considerable magazine, book, and broadcast exposure.

APPROACH TO WRITING

THE BOOKS OF CECIL O. KEMP JR. challenge humanistic philosophies and the wisdom of modern culture.

The core value of loving, caring for, and focusing on God and others is featured in all the books. Relationship with God through faith in Jesus and allowing His Spirit to live within are portrayed as the keys to achieving true greatness: life, relationship, and leadership excellence and success that lasts.

The books offer sound counsel and real hope based on the Bible's unchanging principles of eternal truth. These are embedded in a positive and powerful message that comforts, encourages, heals, instructs, and inspires.

Kemp values what is important in the here and now, and in eternity, for individuals and for the relationship, family, and organization units upon which a caring society and culture rest. Thus he points readers first to spiritual reconciliation, renewal, and restoration, then to selflessness in daily living and working.

He is humbled to have the God-given call, privilege, honor, skills, and resources to produce works of literary distinction that focus on traditional values and contribute an extremely valuable perspective on the genuinely great issues of modern life.

He is proud that his books not only offer a view through the eternal scope and practical, sound solutions that stand the test of time, but openly fly in the face of materialism, intellectualism, man-made religion, and other empty humanistic philosophies.

In promoting the values and priorities of eternal truth that run counter to popular culture, he produces books that are suited for a broad audience—readers of all ages in all places in the world who are open-minded and sincerely searching for what he calls the truly better way of living and working.